THE GUN AND THE LAW

	DATE DUE		

THE GUN AND THE LAW

Joseph Wayne

Chivers Press • G.K. Hall & Co.
Bath, England   Thorndike, Maine USA

This Large Print edition is published by Chivers Press, England, and by G.K. Hall & Co., USA.

Published in 2001 in the U.K. by arrangement with the author c/o Golden West Literary Agency.

Published in 2001 in the U.S. by arrangement with Golden West Literary Agency.

U.K. Hardcover ISBN 0-7540-4485-8   (Chivers Large Print)
U.K. Softcover   ISBN 0-7540-4486-6   (Camden Large Print)
U.S. Softcover   ISBN 0-7838-9418-X   (Nightingale Series Edition)

The text of this Large Print edition is unabridged.
Other aspects of the book may vary from the original edition.

Set in 16 pt. New Times Roman.

Printed in Great Britain on acid-free paper.

British Library Cataloguing in Publication Data available

Library of Congress Cataloging-in-Publication Data

Wayne, Joseph, 1906–
    The gun and the law / by Joseph Wayne.
        p. cm.
    ISBN 0-7838-9418-X (lg. print : sc : alk. paper)
    1. Sheriffs—Fiction. 2. Large type books. I. Title.
PS3529.V33 G77 2001
    813'.54—dc21
                                                    2001016533

CHAPTER ONE

Deputy Sheriff Brady Royal spent the first two hours of the pursuit carefully following trail, figuring that if Lee Spain tried to throw him off it he would do it in the first, swift hours of the chase.

The tracks led south out of Bear Dance, plain and straight as they headed undeviatingly toward the Colorado line. Too plain, too much of an invitation to follow them just long enough to determine their direction and then jump to the conclusion that Spain was trying to reach Colorado where he would be out of the jurisdiction of any Wyoming lawman.

Spain had several hours' start, a fact which made Brady's job an urgent one. But when he found the place where Spain had turned west, he was glad he had taken his time. The trail climbed for six or seven miles through the ragged butte country, then turned again and headed north.

Brady hated Spain as savagely as one man could hate another, but he had to admit Spain was no fool. Spain had been counting on a posse following, not a single man. And from past experience, Spain would certainly have known how a posse worked, particularly when it was composed of excited and outraged men. There was always a certain amount of mob

1

spirit, a strong tendency to guess, to strike out blindly once the fugitive's direction was determined. So a single man, who was a good tracker, might almost be said to have an advantage over a posse.

Once Brady was certain that Spain had reversed his direction, he let his horse out. There was only one way through the mountains north of Bear Dance—the valley of Sundown Creek and on over Sundown Pass. A man and a horse could make it straight up over the rocky peaks if he had to, but a fugitive couldn't afford that much time. Besides, Spain's horse wasn't shod.

Ten miles northwest of Bear Dance, Brady climbed out of the wide valley of Blue Creek, which flowed into Sundown Creek several miles north of town, and came out on a high, rolling plain.

Scrub sagebrush dotted the land, along with the dark red shapes of cattle and those of an occasional band of horses. A dozen antelope watched him curiously from the crest of a ridge, but spooked away as he approached. Brady's eyes scanned the almost limitless horizon ahead, seeing nothing that resembled a man and a horse.

Not that he expected to. The way he figured it, Spain had at least four hours' start. Add to that a couple more hours Brady had lost following trail, and it became a time advantage that probably meant Spain was fifteen or twenty miles ahead.

From the same ridge on which the antelope had stood Brady glanced behind. In the hazy distance he could see the speck that was the clustered buildings of the town of Bear Dance. He could also see the wide valley above the town, the valley that was to have been an irrigated paradise months ago, but which was still unmarked by a stream of water. The main ditch had barely been started.

The irrigation scheme had made nothing but trouble for the Sundown country, and Brady was convinced that out of it had grown the fear and panic that had brought Lee Spain here to kill. Brady believed the man who had hired Spain was Judge Isaac Porter, who had promoted the project from the beginning.

Brady's reasons for suspecting Porter were simple. The promoter was the man who had the most at stake—enough to import a hired killer such as Spain to discourage or put down trouble. But suspecting Porter and proving him guilty in court were two different things. Brady would have to get the truth out of Spain, he told himself, and he would if he had to beat the man half to death.

He rode north, picking the most likely route through the wastes, the route Spain would probably have chosen. But his careful appraisal went unrewarded until late in the afternoon. Then he came upon Spain's trail again, climbing through a gash in a rocky butte. Brady smiled briefly, certain that his guess had been right. Spain was bound for Sundown Pass.

Climbing steadily for several hours through the rising, cedar-covered foothills, Brady hit the first pines at dusk. After that he stopped looking for Spain's trail, relying instead upon his judgment that Spain was headed for the pass.

Likely the man would be so confident he had succeeded in throwing his pursuers off the trail that he would camp tonight, thinking he could safely take the time. On that and on that alone depended Brady's chance of catching him.

Dusk settled upon the land, but not before Brady had chosen his route through the mountains before him. He traveled steadily, resting his horse when he sensed that the animal needed it, and at moonrise dropped into the narrow valley of Sundown Creek and hit the road.

He dismounted and, striking a match, stooped and examined the road carefully, the match cupped in his hands. He did not find Spain's tracks, but failure at this point proved nothing. Spain's route could well have put him onto the road farther north.

Mounting, Brady went on. He was tired, both from nervous tension and from the miles he had put behind, but he gave his weariness no more thought than he did his hunger. If

4

Spain was six hours ahead of him, he could have reached the top of the pass before he camped at dark.

About one in the morning Brady dismounted, picketed his horse and rubbed him down, then stretched out in the grass beside the road; his head pillowed on his saddle. He didn't sleep, but stared wide-eyed at the sky, knowing that if he closed his eyes, weariness would overcome him and he would probably sleep past the first dawn hours and so lose Spain forever.

Strange, he thought, how men's tracks crossed and recrossed during the course of their lives. Take Spain and himself for instance. The man had been a force in Brady's life since Brady was eighteen. Lying there in the chill, high air, Brady felt his body grow hot as memory came rushing back. Anger over the incredibly cruel and senseless thing Spain had done so long ago became a smoldering fire in him once again.

Lee Spain, a complete stranger, had drifted into Brady's home town, a small, out-of-the-way place in Nevada where a man on the dodge could hole up for a while and be reasonably safe. Brady's brother Duane, a year older but weaker and more dependent than Brady, had built Spain into a kind of hero, had taken to following and imitating him. Brady was never really sure what had happened, but he could guess.

Duane's adulation must have first amused, then irritated Spain. He began to needle the boy, about the fuzzy down on his cheeks, about his fear of guns and women. He got Duane drinking, and during one of their sessions he had probably talked too much about his murderous exploits. Then, afraid Duane would talk too much, Spain stirred up a fight between Duane and a drifting saddle tramp when the boy was dizzy with whisky. The fight ended with Duane dead in the dusty street, and the puncher a little puzzled and confused about what had been the cause of the fight . . .

Suddenly Brady realized he was trembling. He remembered he'd gone home, loaded his father's shotgun, and run all the way back to town. The sheriff stopped him as he rushed past the jail. Then the sheriff locked him up and invited Spain to ride.

Spain did, but that wasn't the end. The urge to kill Spain and avenge his brother became the prime purpose in Brady's life. He saved until he could buy a gun. For months he spent everything he made on ammunition and practiced for hours at a time.

When he thought he was ready, he took the trail and lived by the gun, but Spain's path eluded him. Eventually he drifted into Bear Dance and took the deputy's job. And one day Lee Spain also came to Bear Dance.

Now, with the wisdom of hindsight, Brady told himself he should have killed Spain on sight. If he had, Marvin Van Schoen would still be alive. So would his wife and boy. But time had apparently dimmed the once overpowering need for vengeance. So he'd let Spain live, and Spain had done his deadly work.

The old, familiar fury was in Brady again, but with it, was a feeling of guilt about the Van Schoen family—Spain's latest victims.

Like dozens of other farmers, Van Schoen had brought his family to the Sundown country because he had believed Judge Porter's promises. Brady had known Van Schoen well and had liked him. He was honest and hard working, and as long as he had been able to live on his hopes, he had taken great pride in his farm. But, as with many of the other settlers, his hopes had eventually been killed by the countless delays in the construction of Porter's long-promised dams and ditches.

Van Schoen had his share of Dutch stubbornness and courage, qualities which had set him apart from his neighbors. He became a leader, openly criticizing Porter and questioning his intentions and integrity.

If Van Schoen had lived, he eventually would have ruined Porter. Brady was as sure of that as he was sure that the questioning and criticism would die now that Van Schoen was gone. None of the other settlers had the courage to speak up. But being sure of Porter's guilt wasn't proof. For that, he needed Spain's confession . . .

At three Brady rose and saddled his horse. He took a moment to examine the road with a flaring match, and was pleased when he found Spain's tracks, plain and fresh, in the deep dust.

The moon lay far in the west. By its light, Brady could see the slot of Sundown Pass in the ragged peaks ahead. He slowed his horse to a plodding walk and held him in the middle of the road where the dust muffled the sound of his hoofs.

Dawn streaked the eastern horizon with gray, and still the summit lay an hour ahead. But Brady did not hurry. He couldn't afford to alarm Spain or come upon him unexpectedly.

Rose stained the eastern clouds. Glancing left as he rode, Brady saw that the sun was touching the tips of the high peaks, though the bottom of the canyon was still shadowed and cold.

Suddenly the faint odor of smoke reached him, and he knew with a sudden sense of satisfaction that he had reached the end of the hunt.

CHAPTER TWO

Brady reined over to the edge of the road and dismounted in a heavy clump of spruce. He tied his horse and, easing his carbine from the boot, went on up the bed of the creek afoot.

He traveled steadily and with extreme care, moving warily as any skillful hunter would in approaching his prey. He scanned the land ahead, and within ten minutes after he first smelled the smoke, he spotted its rising spiral ahead of him.

Spain was camped in the canyon through which a stream tumbled noisily. Brady left the creek bed and began to climb, aware that he did not have to be as slow and careful as he had been. Here the creek dropped in a series of falls. The pound of the water would drown the small noises he was bound to make.

Spain was very sure of himself, Brady thought, permitting himself the luxury of a fire. He caught his first glimpse of Spain from a rock pile above the fugitive. The sun was at Brady's back, and as he moved into the open, it rose above the high peaks behind him and bathed his back with its thin warmth.

Looking down at the outlaw, Brady felt the old, overpowering hatred rush through him. Coupled with a long-building need to kill this man, it was almost more than he could stand. His hands, white-knuckled with strain, gripped the carbine until they ached. For an instant he lived through that time of over ten years ago, that other time of death, and his helplessness in the face of it. Then, barely controlling himself, he jacked a cartridge into the rifle.

The sound made Spain jump and whirl around. Brady said, 'Don't try it. You know I want to kill you. Don't give me an excuse.'

Spain froze, then continued his turn slowly. His hand, which had dropped to the butt of his holstered gun, fell away deliberately.

Brady said, 'It's up to you whether you go in alive or draped across your saddle. Unbuckle your belt and drop it.'

Spain fumbled with the buckle, his gaze fixed on Brady's face.

Brady's finger tightened on the trigger, and he said softly, 'God knows I've got reason enough to kill you, Spain. Remember that.'

Spain's smile flashed across his dark face. 'You want to, all right, but you won't. Election's coming up and you'll go after the sheriff's job. Trouble is, you've brought too many dead prisoners in already and the people don't like it. And then there's the Ord girl you're fixing to marry. I hear you're a little too quick on the trigger to suit her too.'

Spain stopped abruptly, warned by the new expression in Brady's face. His smile grew strained. He continued to fumble with the buckle as though having trouble with it. He kept his eyes on Brady's face. Suddenly he got his buckle loose and let belt and holstered gun drop to the ground at his feet.

'Another ten seconds,' Brady said, 'and you'd have had a considerable hole in your gut. I'm using soft-nosed hunting bullets in this rifle. I'd like to use one of them on you. Now kick that thing away.'

Spain kicked the gun belt away—about ten feet. Brady walked down the slope, his rifle ready.

Brady was aware that he might be a fool for trying to take a man like Spain in alive. He had already escaped once, undoubtedly helped by Porter or whoever had hired him to murder Van Schoen. He might well escape again before he named the man who had done the hiring.

Vividly Brady remembered the way the Van Schoens had looked lying in front of their house: the man, the woman—a pretty woman with flaxen braids around her head—and the little boy who could not have been much more than ten. But if Brady were to kill Spain, he'd never be able to prove who had hired him, had helped him break jail. And so the man would be free to hire another killer. Men like Spain could always be had for a price.

There was something else, too. When he had first taken the deputy's badge, he had, or so folks said, been too quick on the trigger. Spain had been right in saying Brady had brought in too many dead prisoners to suit the people of Bear Dance. Three, to be exact. He had no regret about any of them, but that wasn't the point.

Number One was a horse thief he had caught east of town. He had the man dead to rights and hadn't expected any trouble, until the thief panicked and started to run. Brady yelled for him to stop and fired a low warning shot. The man stumbled and, falling, caught the bullet in the back of the head.

Number Two was a bank robber. Brady surprised him and his partner here in the pass just below where he'd found Spain. Both men submitted to arrest, but a moment later one of them tried to shoot Brady with a derringer he carried in his boot. Brady shot him, but when they got back to town, the surviving bank robber swore Brady had gunned down an unarmed man.

Number Three was the one people talked about the most. A rancher north of Bear Dance had run off with his neighbor's wife and $500 that belonged to the injured husband. They were within a mile of the Colorado line when Brady caught up with them. The man yelled, 'We're not going back, Royal,' and pulled his gun. Again it was self-defense, but the woman, taking her cue from the bank robber, swore Brady had shot her companion without giving him a chance to surrender. Many people believed her and sympathized with her because they knew she had good reason to leave her husband.

No, Brady had never felt the slightest regret over any of these killings, but he'd got into trouble over them, partly because they had all come within a three month period. Trouble

12

with Shirley Ord, whom he loved. Trouble with her brother, Pete, who was an important man in Bear Dance. Trouble with so many people that he might be defeated if he did run for sheriff at the next election. Well, he'd learned one thing. Take a prisoner in alive and let the law take its course. That was what the people wanted. Or said they did.

Brady said sharply, 'Turn your back to me. Hold your hands together at the back of your neck.'

He fumbled in his pocket for the handcuffs, holding his rifle in one hand, and Spain, moving fast, dived at him, using his head for a ram. He struck Brady in the chest.

Bowled back, Brady still was able to bring the steel handcuffs down in a cutting, clubbing motion. They slashed across Spain's face, bringing a rush of blood. Then Brady was on his back in the rocks and Spain was grappling with him for the rifle.

A savage satisfaction took hold of Brady, releasing all the outrage and fury that had festered inside him through the years. Deliberately he tore the rifle from Spain's grasp and threw it into the creek. His knee slammed into Spain's groin, and the outlaw bellowed with pain, doubled up and rolled away.

Brady got to his feet. His face was skinned by the rocky ground; his lungs labored for air, but his eyes were bright with satisfaction. 'You

13

want it this way, so you'll get it this way. I hoped you'd make a stab at it, Spain. By God, I hoped you would.'

Spain got to his knees, his face gray. He hung his head as though spent, then suddenly came lunging up and forward, driving his body against Brady's knees.

As Brady went back, he brought his clasped hands down like a club against the back of Spain's neck. The outlaw's face skidded across the rock-strewn ground. Brady staggered away, fighting for footing. Then, having gained it, he stepped forward. 'Get up. Get up, or do you want me to kick you to death?'

Spain rose, shaking his head, a rock in each hand. He moved toward Brady, weaving and feinting like a prize fighter. Brady moved in quickly, like a wolf to the kill. His fists slashed at Spain's face, hammering the man to the ground. Brady leaped astride him.

'This is some different from the day you killed the Van Schoens, isn't it, Spain? You don't do so good against someone who fights back. Now tell me. You did kill them, didn't you?'

Spain nodded, his eyes dull with pain. 'Yeah. Yeah, I killed 'em. Now let up, will you?'

'Who hired you?'

'Go to hell. I need him worse than you do.'

Brady poised a heavy fist. Spain winced, but kept silent. Brady lowered his fist, knowing he could beat Spain insensible and the man would

14

never talk. He pushed himself away, sweating and spent. He could not remember ever wanting so desperately to kill. The very intensity of his desire frightened him. Maybe the townspeople were right about him being trigger happy, maybe Shirley Ord was right about him not being honestly convinced that law should be enforced through the courts.

'All right,' he said, 'get up. Get on your horse before I finish what I started.'

Spain rolled over, groaning, then finally he struggled to his feet. Brady followed him, watching while Spain saddled up. Coming back to the campsite, he picked up Spain's gun and belt and slung them over his shoulders.

'Get on your horse,' he told Spain. 'Ride downstream. Try kicking that animal into a run and you'll be dead before he hits a trot.'

Spain rode out at a walk, Brady following. In less than ten minutes they reached his horse. He untied the animal and mounted stiffly, his body one great ache from the beating he had taken.

Brady let Spain lead down the canyon road, then after they had covered a hundred yards he rode up and took the reins from him. After that he led Spain's horse.

The temptation to let his prisoner ride ahead all the way to town had been a strong one. Sooner or later Spain would have made a break. If he had, Brady would have had to kill him.

But regardless of how he felt about Spain, he had to do this right. He had to prove to the town, and to himself, that he wasn't a killer masquerading behind a badge.

CHAPTER THREE

Brady Royal brought Lee Spain into Bear Dance early in the afternoon of July 6th. The day was a blistering one here in the Sundown Creek valley, and Brady showed what forty-eight hours in the saddle—without sleep, without even a decent meal—could do to a man.

He hadn't shaved since the evening of July 3rd. His beard stubble, ordinarily black, had been turned gray by the high plains dust that lay like a mask on his bruised face. Sore-muscled from his fight with Spain and tired to the point of exhaustion, he could still feel a grim satisfaction. Few had expected him to bring Spain in at all, and probably no one in Bear Dance had expected him to bring Spain in alive. Well, he'd done his job. This time nobody could criticize him for being trigger happy.

Spain was considerably worse off than Brady. His face resembled a chunk of beef that had been left out in the sun to rot. One eye was swelled almost shut, and beneath it was the deep gash made by Brady's handcuffs at the start of the fight. His lips were puffy, his nose flattened, but his eyes were as virulent as ever.

Entering Bear Dance's short business block, Spain straightened in his saddle and lifted his head defiantly. Probably only Brady sensed the quick panic that was in him as he glimpsed the scaffold that had been erected the year before at the far end of the street.

Brady thought. He'll talk when I put a rope around his neck. He won't die without talking.

Brady was human enough to look for approval in the faces of the people who had lined the walks to stare at the pair as they rode toward the jail. He was puzzled when he failed to find it. Their faces only showed disapproval and anger, which they made no effort to conceal.

Brady guessed what they were thinking. They might just as well have said it in words: 'You've been free with your gun ever since you got the deputy's job here. You've killed three men, but Spain is the worst one who ever hit town and you bring him in alive. Why?' And Brady realized he couldn't really answer the question to their satisfaction. Too much of his reason was personal, and nobody was likely to believe it anyway.

A group of Judge Porter's settlers stood in front of Ord's Mercantile. They were a ragged, beaten-looking lot. Brady could guess why they

17

were here. They had been asking Pete Ord for credit, and, as usual, getting refused.

Everyone in town knew the settlers were finished. By this time they must have known it themselves. They'd never be able to meet the payments on their notes to Porter because they couldn't make a crop even if the dam was finished this year. Starved out, they'd have to leave, surrendering the land they'd bought from Porter, losing everything they had paid for it.

Van Schoen had claimed that was Porter's plan, that he had purposely delayed construction on one pretext or another. The dam was to have been finished in March, but here it was July and neither the dam nor ditches were finished. According to Van Schoen, Porter intended all the time to starve the settlers out so he could sell the land next year to a new bunch of suckers. Van Schoen had repeated his charge often and loudly, and now Van Schoen was dead.

Pete Ord stepped out on the veranda of the Mercantile, his sister Shirley behind him. Brady looked longest at Shirley, trying to make out the expression on her face and failing because she was partly hidden by the crowd.

Anger stirred in Brady as he saw the same disapproving glare on Pete Ord's face he had seen on so many others along the street. Well, you were damned if you did, and damned if you didn't. He'd been criticized by nearly

18

everyone in town because he'd been too ready to use his gun. Now he'd be condemned because he hadn't used it.

His anger mounting, Brady looked up to the window of Judge Porter's office over the bank. Porter stood at the window, leaning out slightly, his hands on the window sill.

Porter was tall, tanned, and white-haired. The most distinguished-looking man in Bear Dance. Persuasive, too. Brady had often thought wryly that Porter could sell a drowning man a drink of water. Now Porter was scowling as his eyes shifted from Brady's and came to rest on two of his men across the street. One was Courtney, his burly, bearded construction foreman. The other was Lund, squat as a toad and almost as ugly. Brady had often wondered about him. All he knew about the man was that he was Courtney's constant side-kick.

A third man, a stranger who called himself Dude Vedder, stood beside Courtney. Brady was curious about him, too. He said he came from California. Maybe he had, for he wore Mexican clothes which were common there, but out of place in Wyoming.

Frowning, Brady trailed Spain past the bank. He saw Spain look up at Porter, his gaze holding until Porter was behind them, then he glanced back at Brady and grinned. After that the outlaw rode with his head high, his look of open contempt touching one person after another on the sun-washed street.

19

Brady felt the flow of undercurrents around him, the hatred of the townspeople and settlers for Spain, their dislike of Brady because Spain was alive. But there was more, something between Porter and Spain. If he could only prove a connection between them . . .

Spain had drifted into town two weeks before. Five days ago he'd had a wrangle with Van Schoen in town. Brady had broken it up, but not until Van Schoen had made some threats. Later that night Brady had heard Van Schoen was dead, and had ridden out to find the three of them sprawled on the ground in front of their shack . . .

They rode on toward the courthouse at the end of the block. It stood on a grassy square, a two-story frame building, its paint long gone under the eroding impact of Wyoming's dust and sun and wind. It was the tallest building in town, with its bell cupola, and the most neglected. The lawn hadn't been cut or watered all summer. A single cottonwood, shedding cotton into the still air, relieved only slightly its bleak monotony.

Brady pulled up at the long hitch pole in front of the courthouse, dismounted and tied Spain's horse, then his own. He motioned to Spain. 'Get down, damn you. Get a move on.'

Spain swung down stiffly and walked toward the courthouse door. Brady followed.

Spain turned his head toward Brady as they

reached the steps. 'What's the sense of this, Deputy? I'll never come to trial and you know it.'

Brady thought of his brother, of Van Schoen and his wife and boy, twisted and still and bloody on the dusty ground. 'Get up those steps,' he said, 'before I kick your guts out.'

Shrugging, Spain climbed the steps. 'All right. I'll get me a few hours' sleep and a couple of meals on the county, then I'll be out again. Wait and see.' His eyes grew hard and still. 'Come after me again and you'll be dead.'

Brady followed him up the steps, unable to shake his feeling of uneasiness. Someone had smuggled Spain a gun before, and in spite of Brady's and the sheriff's precautions it could happen again.

Spain stopped at the top of the spur-scarred steps. Brady put a hand on Spain's back and shoved roughly. Spain staggered through the door, into the cool corridor. He turned toward the sheriff's office without being told and went in.

Frank Bowie, the sheriff, rose from where he sat at his desk in the corner, nodded at Brady without enthusiasm. 'So you got him.'

'Yeah, I got him. Lock him up.' Brady dropped wearily into the nearest chair. 'I guess he's hungry, Frank.'

'I'll send for a meal.' Bowie opened the heavy iron door that led into the jail corridor. 'You know the way, Spain.'

Brady watched until they disappeared, Bowie limping stiffly on his game left leg. He'd stopped a bullet a couple of years ago when he and Brady had run down a couple of horse thieves in the buttes southwest of Bear Dance. The slug had smashed his knee cap, angling up into his thigh. The cap hadn't healed right and his leg wasn't much good any more, so he was sitting out the rest of his term, letting Brady do the running. He was fifty-five, too old to start a new career. It didn't bother him, though. He'd never been a man to worry.

Bowie returned a moment later. Going to the hall door, he bellowed to the janitor, 'Luke! Fetch some dinner for Spain.'

He came back and, sitting down at his desk, gingerly lifted his tooled boots to its top. He put his sharp blue eyes on Brady as he picked up his pipe and dribbled tobacco into it. 'Tell me about it,' he said.

'Not much to tell. You figured he'd go for the Colorado line, and he was counting on us figuring that. He left a straight plain trail for damn near ten miles. Then he hit a stretch of hardpan and swung west through the buttes. I was onto him after that and careful, so I didn't have much trouble finding where he turned north. I rode all night and came up with him at dawn. He was so sure he'd outsmarted me he even had a fire going.'

The sheriff tamped tobacco into the bowl of his pipe, then lighted it, his eyes not leaving

Brady's face for an instant. He looked older than he was, Brady thought, with his white hair and droopy white mustache, his lined and leathery face.

Frank Bowie had carried the star in this county for more than twenty years. He'd seen the valley change from wilderness to the way it was now, with Judge Porter's settlers dotting the flat with their shacks. He'd seen trouble, and now he was watching it develop again.

His honesty and courage had never been questioned, even by his enemies. But he was an old-time lawman, another of the gun-law advocates and, as with Brady, he'd come in for his share of criticism because he believed an officer should be judge, jury and executioner all rolled into one. It was an opinion he had held from the time he'd first pinned on a star more than thirty years ago, and he wasn't about to change.

'Looks like you knocked him around some,' Bowie said.

Brady nodded, knowing what was coming. 'He gave me a little trouble, but before I got done, he admitted the killings. He wouldn't say who hired him, but I figure he'll tell us when we put the rope around his neck.'

Bowie leaned forward and pulled steadily on his pipe. He studied the scuffed toe of his boot. 'He got out once, with some help. He may again. When he resisted arrest, you should have killed him.'

Brady deliberately rolled and lighted a cigarette. 'You know why I didn't, Frank. No use going over it again.'

Bowie's eyes held Brady's steadily. 'A year ago you'd have fetched Spain in draped across his saddle.'

'Maybe. But I've learned something in the last year, Frank. It's not the sheriff's job to decide a man's guilt. They have judges and juries for that.'

Bowie grinned ruefully. 'You're gambling, Brady. Next year you'll run for sheriff. Whether you get it or not depends on how many voters subscribe to your notions. A lot of 'em talk it, but I doubt like hell that many of 'em will vote the way they talk.'

'Maybe I won't run.'

'The hell you won't. I trained you for the job. Besides, you're the best man for it, although I don't mind telling you I don't like the way you handled Spain.'

Brady threw down his cigarette. 'You know I wanted to kill him, but that's the trouble. The law's supposed to be impersonal. It doesn't give me the right to kill Spain because of my brother or because of the Van Schoens. Shirley and her brother Pete and damned near everybody else in the county have cussed me for being trigger-happy too long. Now they're going to get the law enforced their way whether they like it or not. And there's another thing. I want the man who paid Spain.

24

He'll talk when we put the noose over his head.'

'You figure it's Porter?'

'Has to be. Who else wanted Van Schoen out of the way?'

Bowie stared at him with exaggerated patience. 'Son, you're twenty-nine years old. Time you stopped dreaming about the way things ought to be and took a good look at the way they are. Spain won't talk. I know his kind. He'll let on that he will to scare Porter into breaking him out again, but when it comes to the showdown, it ain't in him to tattle on the one who hired him.'

The sheriff picked up his pipe again. 'If it is Porter who hired him, and the chances are you're right, we'd better see to it that Spain don't get plugged. That'd be a hell of a lot easier way to keep his mouth shut than busting him out again.'

'I thought of that,' Brady admitted. 'Well, we'll just have to keep our eyes open.' He rose. 'I'm all in, Frank. I'm going to get dinner and then sleep the clock around.'

He left the room, walking along the hall and out into the hot sunlight, more worried than he wanted Bowie to know. Porter had a fortune at stake. The way Brady saw it, Porter had been desperate enough to hire Spain to murder the Van Schoens, at least Marvin Van Schoen, who had been kicking up all the fuss. Then he'd been desperate enough to smuggle

25

a gun to Spain, although Brady still wasn't sure how it had been done.

Now Porter would certainly know that Spain was a threat to his future, even to his life. If Porter had gone this far, he would not be above finding a way to shut Spain's mouth permanently.

Walking slowly to his horse, Brady wished Spain's trial could start tomorrow. But at best the machinery of law was slow—damned slow. All that he and Frank Bowie could do was guard Spain day and night. He had to be kept alive long enough to be tried and hanged, and that, he thought bitterly, was the last thing the people of Bear Dance wanted. A trial meant a jury, and that meant some people would have to take sides against Judge Porter's man. And yet these same people were dependent on Porter for their homes, their livelihood. It was Brady's guess that the good people of Bear Dance would be happier if Spain were murdered in his cell tonight.

CHAPTER FOUR

Brady paused at the hitchrail and made another cigarette. Luke, the janitor, crossed the street on a long diagonal course straight from the restaurant, a tray in his hands. He went into the courthouse with it, nodding at

Brady as he passed.

Still Brady did not move. He knew he should get his dinner and go to bed, but a curious lethargy was upon him, a reluctance to move. The sun was hot on his back, and he puffed lazily on the cigarette.

Luke came out of the courthouse again and headed toward the bank. Brady watched him idly as he went upstairs over the bank where Porter's office was located. He came out again in a few minutes and returned to the courthouse. Brady stopped him and asked, 'Spain send for Porter?'

Luke, an elderly, shuffling man with a drooping mustache that was perpetually stained with chewing tobacco, nodded. Brady watched him disappear into the courthouse. He considered Spain's move. No doubt he'd lay it on the line. Porter would break him out again or he'd talk. At least Porter would promise to break him out. How and when he'd make his try were questions Brady couldn't answer, but one thing was sure. Brady or Frank Bowie would be in the sheriff's office from now until Lee Spain was hanged.

Brady untied his horse and stiffly swung into the saddle. He reined around and headed toward the bank. Reaching it, he stepped down. Porter's two men, Courtney and Lund, were leaning against the front wall of the bank building. They were talking to the newcomer, Dude Vedder.

Vedder was a dark-skinned, slender young man probably not over nineteen or twenty. He carried two pearl-handled .44's, butts forward for a cross-body draw. Brady had never seen him pull a gun, but if the man's supple grace in other things was any indication, he'd be fast.

Brady smiled wryly. Hell, a man carrying fancy hardware like that would have to be fast or he'd be hoorawed out of the country in no time.

Brady tied his horse and stepped onto the walk. Vedder spat at his feet.

'What's your trouble?' Brady asked evenly.

Vedder grinned at him, then glanced at Courtney and Lund as though for support. Finding none in their stony faces, he turned back to Brady. 'No trouble. Only it looks to me like this country needs a new sheriff. A new deputy, too. One that knows his job.'

'Like you, maybe?' Brady asked softly.

Vedder's face flushed. He didn't reply, but he kept staring at Brady, his dark eyes turning a little wild when he heard Courtney's mocking chuckle.

Brady studied him. He knew the kind. The youth was fighting his age, and doing it with bluff and bravado. But there was more to him than that. He was dangerous because he was unstable, and this instability warned Brady that Vedder's actions would be unpredictable and not always rational.

'A crippled sheriff and a yellow deputy,'

Vedder muttered. 'Ain't that a combination for you?'

'Vedder, don't push,' Brady said, his voice still soft.

'Why not? You goin' to shoot me, maybe?'

Brady felt a wildness rising in him, a wildness he thought he had put behind him. He realized that his hands, in spite of being clenched, were trembling. He looked deliberately at Courtney and Lund. 'This your party?'

Courtney, always the spokesman for the pair, shook his head. 'We're just standin' here.'

Brady brought his gaze back to Vedder, fighting himself for control. He couldn't afford to let a kid like Dude Vedder suck him into a gunfight, and that was exactly what the fellow was trying to do.

'If you're looking for trouble, you're jumping the wrong man,' Brady said. 'I'll throw you into the jug so fast you won't know what happened.'

'On what charge, Deputy?' Vedder demanded. 'For speakin' my mind? You goin' to jail everyone that don't like the way you operate? If you are, you'd better get busy 'cause that takes in most of the town.'

'You make a lot of big talk, Vedder. See that it stays just talk. You draw a gun in Bear Dance and you'll answer to me. The best thing I could do for you would be to make you watch Spain hang, and that's what I'll do.'

Vedder stepped back, his hands jerking out from under his belt. 'I ain't like Spain,' he said shrilly. 'I wouldn't kill a woman and a kid, but I'll kill a man. Any time. Any time you say.'

Brady knew he had Vedder tagged. 'You're a two-bit imitation of a bad man, Vedder,' Brady said.

He shouldered past Vedder toward the building entrance, presenting his broad, sweat-and-dust-stained back to Vedder, who stood motionless for a moment until Brady disappeared inside.

'You seen him,' Vedder said to Courtney, his voice high and thin. 'He ain't so damn tough.'

'Why didn't you take him?' Courtney asked.

'For nothin'? You'd like that, wouldn't you? So would your fancy boss.'

'Shut up,' Courtney said, and turned away. 'Come on, Lund. I'll buy you a drink.'

Vedder caught his arm. 'Listen,' he said, his mouth twitching furiously. 'I want to work for you. I faced the deputy down, didn't I? Don't that prove somethin'?'

'Sure. It proves you're a damn fool. Did you know Brady Royal has killed three men since he started wearing the star in this county?'

Vedder ignored the question. 'Porter ain't got Spain any more. He's goin' to need a good man. Besides, Spain's likely to talk when they put that noose around his neck.'

Courtney swung back and took a step

forward until he stood within three feet of Vedder. 'Talk? About what?'

Vedder missed the expression on Courtney's face, the tone of his voice. He said eagerly, ' 'Bout Porter hirin' him to kill Van Schoen. He won't keep still when—'

Courtney's heavy, open hand struck the side of Vedder's face with an impact that could be heard across the street. The blow sent the slight-bodied Vedder spinning off the sidewalk and onto his knees in the dust of the street.

Vedder scrambled up and fell into a crouch, cursing, but he didn't reach for either gun. Lund's revolver covered him.

'Royal was right,' Courtney said contemptuously. 'You sure need dryin' behind the ears. Now get out of here. If you start shootin' off your mouth again, I'll kill you.'

Vedder looked at the gun in Lund's hand, at the expressionless eyes above it. He licked his lips and rubbed his hands against the sides of his pants. Then he reluctantly swung around and stalked off toward the livery stable.

Lund replaced his gun, glancing at Courtney. 'We ought to kill him. He's likely to start talking again.'

Courtney shook his head. 'Not yet. Porter might be able to use him.'

With that, he crossed the street, leaving the squat Lund to trot along behind at his heels.

*   *   *

31

Wearily Brady climbed the stairs in the bank building to Porter's office. Damn it, he'd been in the saddle forty-eight hours. He was hungry and he needed to sleep the clock around, but curiosity nagged at him. He wanted to see Porter, wanted to know what the man would have to say.

Porter was leaving his office just as Brady reached the top of the stairs. He was wearing a white linen suit that showed off his darkly tanned face and shining white hair and mustache with maximum effect.

Porter smiled warmly when he saw Brady. 'A fine job, Mr. Royal, bringing Spain in. Fine.'

'I understand Spain sent for you.'

Porter nodded. 'I assume he wants to retain me since I'm the only lawyer in town.'

'Taking the job?'

Porter frowned judiciously. 'I don't see how I can. I'll talk to him, of course, but I can't actually represent him. He killed three of my people, you know. At least he's accused of killing them.'

'He did it all right,' Brady said. 'He admitted he did.'

Porter had a talent for hiding his feelings, but now for a brief instant Brady thought the man's eyes showed worry. Then the expression was gone and he asked casually, 'Did he say anything else?'

'No, but he will when we put that noose

around his neck. He won't hang alone.'

'You think someone hired him to kill the Van Schoens? Why on earth would anyone hire a man to kill a woman and child. A man, perhaps, but not . . .'

'Let's quit trying to fool each other, Judge,' Brady said. 'You hired Spain because Van Schoen was the one man among the settlers who had the guts to buck you. He'd become a leader and the rest were listening. If he'd kept on, he'd have ruined your little scheme. But you're right about the woman and boy. Why were they killed?'

Porter's handsome face grew florid. 'Damn it, I won't tolerate your accusations. By God, I won't. Not after what I've done for this community.'

'After what you've done?' Brady asked softly. He was puzzled by Porter's reaction, for he saw a blustering fury in the man he had never seen before. Then, his gaze meeting Porter's, he understood. The promoter's eyes were hard and ruthless, reflecting none of the rage he was trying to convince Brady that he felt. He was acting and doing a good job of it. Most men would have been indignant at Brady's accusations, and Porter thought that was the pose he ought to take. The truth was, Isaac Porter was a cool customer, and a tough one.

Porter shouted, 'That's what I said. I have done a great deal for this community and I intend to do more.'

'What do you figure on doing about my accusations?' Brady asked.

'I'll have you fired. You're not an elected official, Mr. Royal. You're hired by the sheriff. He won't have any trouble replacing you.'

'With Courtney? Or Lund? You've got influence, is that it? Or maybe you'll handle me the way you took care of Van Schoen?'

Brady expected Porter to rage some more, but he dropped his role of the indignant man. He stood very straight; his eyes narrowed slightly as he studied Brady. He said, 'I do have influence. I'll have a talk with Frank Bowie. There are other men in this county who will talk to Bowie, too. Men like Pete Ord.'

He was right about that, and it angered Brady. 'Now I'll tell you something, Judge. Van Schoen was right about your scheme being a swindle. Bowie and me can't touch you for that, but we'll get you for murder. You'll hang from the same scaffold Spain swings from. You hear that?'

'Can you prove anything against me?' Porter asked. 'Anything?'

'Not yet, but I will before I'm through. Now get my damn job if you can.'

Brady turned and stamped down the stairs. Porter was his man. If he'd had any doubt before, it was gone now. For the first time he had caught a glimpse of the cold and brutal ruthlessness that was in Isaac Porter, and he knew now the man was even more dangerous than he had supposed.

CHAPTER FIVE

After Brady left, Porter stood looking down the empty stairs. He *would* get the man fired. He'd better.

He walked back through the door into his office and sat down in the swivel chair behind his roll-top desk. He leaned forward and struck the desk with his fist. The deputy knew. He admitted he didn't have proof but he said he'd get it, and he was the kind who might.

Damn Spain for bungling a simple job. He had been hired to kill Marvin Van Schoen, and if he'd done only that, everything would be all right. It had been planned so carefully. He'd had Spain get into a drunken quarrel with Van Schoen over something which had no connection with the irrigation project. He'd told Spain to get abusive. He had, and the scheme had worked out precisely as Porter had planned. Enraged, Van Schoen had threatened Spain.

All Spain had to do after that was to catch Van Schoen away from home, and kill him and claim self-defense. If he had followed orders, everything would have been all right, but no,

35

Spain was the kind who liked to see people suffer, so he'd gone out to the Van Schoen farm to watch him crawl when he sobered up and realized whom he had threatened.

Porter didn't know exactly what had happened, but he could guess. Spain had killed Van Schoen in cold blood, and Mrs. Van Schoen and the boy had witnessed the murder. At any rate, all three of them were dead. But worst and most stupid of all, Spain had ridden away on a horse with a split hoof which had left a track as easily identified as a signature.

For a time he stared at the shiny surface of the mahogany desk before him, Then, gradually, his intelligence began to bring reason out of chaos. First, he carefully assessed Spain's character. The man wouldn't talk now. He probably wouldn't say anything during his trial. But he might, under pressure.

Porter was positive he had a little time. How much he wasn't sure. Whatever move he made would have to come within the next few days. There were two possibilities. One was getting Spain out of jail again.

If Spain had another chance at freedom, he'd go far and fast enough not to be caught. But how could it be worked? It had been easy enough for Courtney to slip a gun to Spain before because nobody had been expecting it; but this time they'd be watching Spain every hour out of the twenty-four. Royal or the sheriff or both would be in the sheriff's office day and night.

The other possibility was to kill Spain while he was still in jail. Porter leaned back in his chair giving this careful study. It was one sure way of keeping Spain from talking, but it might not be the safest. Still, maybe it would be smart to run the risk. As long as Spain was alive, he was dangerous to Porter's future.

He stood up. He'd talk to Courtney and Lund and then decide. Spain had asked to see him, so he'd have an excuse to talk to the man. He'd reassure Spain, make any promise the fellow wanted, and that would buy the time he needed.

He crossed the room and, taking his wide-brimmed, cream-colored hat from the tree, went out into the hall. His hand went up automatically to smooth his sweeping mustache. A smile, unctuous and benign, fixed itself on his face. With great dignity he went down the stairs and into the street.

'Judge' was a title of respect that Porter had skillfully introduced upon first arriving here. He had never been a judge, but he hoped someday to become one. He was well on the way to it, too.

He had cleaned up on this first bunch of settlers. With money collected from them, he had paid off all he owed on the land in Sundown Valley. He had paid for the small amount of work he'd felt he must do on the dam and ditch system. He had provided his wife with a wardrobe suitable to their position here, and he had leased the most pretentious house in town.

Two more years, according to his plan. Two more years and two more crops of settlers. He'd have enough money then. And he'd regain the country's respect when he completed the dam and ditches and put water onto the flat. All the harsh things the doubters had said about him, all the suspicions, would vanish.

Nodding genially to right and left, he walked with dignified grace along the street toward the courthouse. He saw himself being elected as county judge, then circuit judge. He smiled, filled with satisfaction as he visualized himself wearing the robes of justice of the supreme court.

Then the courthouse came into view and his face clouded. Lee Spain was still his problem. Lee Spain could spoil everything. Somehow, someway, Spain had to be removed.

He climbed the courthouse steps and entered the gloomy corridor that smelled of disinfectant. He went on into the sheriff's office near the end of the hall. Frank Bowie was inside, sitting behind his cluttered desk thoughtfully sucking the stem of a dead pipe. Frank's feet were on the desk, but they came down as Porter stepped through the door.

Porter inspected Bowie's face carefully, hiding his feelings behind a genial smile. Had

Royal been bluffing? Did Bowie, too, suspect him of complicity in the Van Schoen murders?

Bowie's face was bland, his eyes respectful. 'Come to see Spain, Judge?'

Porter nodded, feeling more confident. The suspicions had been Brady's alone. Frank Bowie wasn't shrewd enough to put that kind of look on his face unless he honestly respected and admired a man.

'Of course I can't represent him,' Porter said. 'You understand how that is. He's accused of killing some of my people out on the flat and it just wouldn't do for me to defend him. But I thought that in all justice I should see him. Perhaps I can recommend a lawyer from some other town.'

'Sure, Judge. I understand.' Bowie got up. The jail keys were upon a chain secured to his belt. Jangling them, he preceded the judge into a jail corridor and along it until he reached Lee Spain's cell. 'Want to go in? Or stay out here?'

Porter stared at Spain. The man looked like a caged, wounded animal. Porter knew he had nothing to fear from the outlaw, but it might look better if he acted as though he thought he had. He said, 'Out here, if you don't mind, Sheriff. Not that I'm afraid, but . . .'

Bowie chuckled. 'Course not. Just good sense is all.' He turned and walked away, the keys still jangling. He called back, 'If you need me, holler. You'll have to raise your voice, though. Won't carry to my office unless you yell.'

Porter waited until Bowie was back in his office. Then he said in a low tone, 'You fool. You had your chance and missed it.'

Spain rose from the bunk and sauntered across the cell to the bars. He grinned at the judge, taunting him. 'I'll have another chance. You're smart enough to see that I do.'

'How can I do that? The first time was easy because they didn't expect anything. But from now on they'll be watching you every minute.'

Spain's eyes hardened. 'It's your job to figure out a way. You will, too, because you know what will happen if you don't.'

'Nobody will believe what you say.'

'Nobody?' Spain shook his head, grinning. 'Brady Royal will. He's counting on me talking. You might be surprised how many others will, too. Ever see a lynch mob, Judge? Take a look at your hungry settlers next time you go out into the street. They don't like you. Van Schoen talked too much before I got to him.'

Porter felt his skin turn clammy, and it angered him. 'All right! I'll take care of you. Just sit tight until I do. And keep your mouth shut.'

Spain stood there looking at him, grinning a little, and Porter had the feeling that Spain was looking through and deep beyond his dignified exterior. He fumbled for a cigar, nearly dropped it, then put it into his mouth and bit off the end.

'Send me a box of those cigars, Judge,' Spain said.

'You know I can't do that.'

Spain looked at him as though he were a butterfly pinned to a cork. 'Send me some.'

'All right, I'll see what I can do.' Porter took a long breath. 'Why the devil did you kill the woman—and the kid? I told you Van Schoen.'

'They saw me do it, that's why. I thought I had Van Schoen alone, but they came runnin' out of the house right after I shot him. Nothin' else I could do.'

Porter's stomach muscles began to twitch. The man was a fool. Why hadn't he made sure Van Schoen was alone? He said, 'I'll get the cigars to you,' and swung on his heel.

'Just a minute, Judge.' As Porter turned around to face him, Spain spat through the bars onto the corridor floor. 'Porter, you don't give a damn about anybody's hide but your own. Just in case you get the bright idea that it'd be safe to shut my mouth for good, I'll tell you something. I wrote the whole business down and mailed it to a friend of mine in Cheyenne. How you first contacted me and how much you paid me and why you wanted Van Schoen beefed.' He waggled a dirty forefinger at Porter. 'The minute my friend hears I'm dead, he'll mail the statement to Bowie, so you'd better see to it I stay mighty

41

damned healthy.'

Without a word, Porter walked down the corridor and into the sheriff's office. He studied Bowie's face a moment, but could read nothing there. He said, 'Spain's a bad one, Sheriff. A real bad one. I doubt if any lawyer can do anything . . .'

'Don't worry about it, Judge,' Bowie said. 'The county will see he's represented.'

'Yes, of course.'

Porter nodded ponderously and went on into the hall and along it until he reached the door. He paused on the courthouse steps, wondering if Spain had been bluffing about his friend, and realizing that he couldn't risk ignoring the threat. Besides, Spain was no fool . . .

The sun hung low in the western sky, but the heat was as great as it had been in the middle of the day. He took a linen handkerchief from his pocket and wiped his face. As he glanced across the street and toward town, he saw Courtney and Lund standing in front of the Red Dog Saloon.

He walked down the steps and, angling across the street, stopped in front of the Red Dog. He spoke to Courtney whom he knew to be the more intelligent of the two. Courtney was supposed to be a construction man and something of an engineer, but he was far from it. He had built a couple of brush-and-dirt-filled dams, but he wasn't qualified for a job as big as the one Porter had promised Sundown Valley.

On the other hand he was, with Lund, Porter's man Friday and ideal for his purpose. He could handle simple construction; he had no moral scruples; and, possessing both great physical strength and an overbearing kind of courage, he was equipped to handle anything that came up.

He could have taken care of Van Schoen without making the mistakes Spain had. Porter had thought about it and decided against using him because he'd be needed here for at least two more years, and Porter hadn't wanted to risk losing him. Still, it would have been better than importing Spain. Porter had bought loyalty of a sort from Courtney and Lund by promising them ten per cent of the project, loyalty that nothing could buy from Lee Spain.

'I want to talk to you, Courtney,' Porter said. 'In my office.'

'Lund, too?'

'Of course. I'll meet you there in five minutes.'

He went into the saloon and ordered a beer. It was cold and his throat was dry. He felt immeasurably refreshed when he left.

Crossing the street, he climbed the stairs to his office. He closed the door behind him, the benign mask dropping from his face. 'We've got to get Spain out again,' he said.

'The hell,' Courtney said. 'Let him rot in

jail. We got him out once and look what happened. He don't deserve another chance.'

'I agree,' Porter said. 'I have no more use for him than you have. But he's threatening to talk. And in case you're thinking about killing him, forget it. Spain has us stopped there.' And he told them how.

'So he talks,' Courtney said. 'Well, you hired him, Judge. We didn't.'

Porter sat down at his desk, knowing there was only one way to handle men like these. He understood them far better than he understood a professional killer like Lee Spain. He busied himself for a time with his cigar, then said deliberately, 'You were both present when I hired him, which makes you as guilty as I am. What's more, you're part of the company, which means that you will share the responsibility as well as the profits.'

'You get ninety per cent and we get ten per cent which we split,' Courtney said. 'And for that we all run the same risk of hanging. Is that it?'

'That's the size of it,' Porter said.

He thought the big foreman was going to argue, but he didn't. Courtney shrugged and said, 'Hell, no use fighting about it. If Spain names you, it'll cook the rest of us too. Likely them plow pushers out on the flat won't wait for a trial. They'll string us all up together. All right, you're supposed to be the brains of the outfit. How do we get Spain out?'

Porter frowned. 'Don't you know of someone who isn't connected with us? It would be better if you boys were somewhere else when it—'

'Vedder,' Lund broke in.

Courtney chuckled. 'Sure. 'Why didn't I think of him?'

'Who is Vedder?'

'A punk,' Courtney said. 'Thinks he's a gun sharp, but I figure he's just crazy enough to do it.'

It was all Porter wanted. He said, 'Find him, but don't mention my name. Tell him it's worth five hundred if he gets Spain out. If he agrees, it's up to you boys to see that Spain has the best damn horse in the country, grub, guns, and plenty of ammunition. That clear?'

Courtney and Lund nodded. Porter rose, and opened a small safe in the corner, and took out a handful of bills. He handed them to Courtney. 'Give him two-fifty now and the rest of it when he gets Spain out of jail.'

Lund's cold stare reminded Porter of a malignant toad. But Courtney nodded and took the money. He said, 'The punk may get killed trying, but he's the kind who'll sure try. He hit us up for a job not more'n an hour ago.' He grinned. 'I hope Brady Royal is guarding Spain when Vedder goes in after him.'

'Why?' Porter asked.

'Well, Vedder loves Royal just like I do,' Courtney said, and, motioning to Lund to follow, left the room.

Porter watched them go, realizing that he shared Courtney's hope. He was still smarting from the things the deputy had said to him earlier in the afternoon. If Royal was still alive when this was over, he'd take care of him, someway. He had to.

He sat down at his desk again, reflecting that Vedder would be lucky to get half of the five hundred. Courtney and Lund would split anything they could hold out. But that was all right if the job was done. There was some danger of them involving him if anything went sour. He might have to pay a good deal more than the five hundred before he was out of this, but he was prepared to pay. Right now the only thing he wanted was to get Spain out of the country. He never wanted to see the man again, wanted to forget, if possible, that Spain had ever existed.

He sat there in his swivel chair for a long time, staring out of the window, watching the sunlight die as the sun dropped behind the ragged horizon in the west, his mind busy with his plans. Then, in early twilight, he got up and went down the street.

He walked home slowly, wondering if Vedder would do his job tonight. He hoped so. The sooner the better. He wanted it finished, wanted to forget all about it.

His house usually pleased him when he rounded the corner and saw it standing there, surrounded by a well-kept lawn, with the great elm and white picket fence. It looked solid, respectable, exactly the way a judge's house should look, unassailable and above the attacks of small men like Brady Royal.

But tonight the sight of the house gave him little pleasure. If only Marian were happier here. Well, she'd have to give him two more years. That was all he'd need. After that they'd be able to leave if she still wanted to. They'd be able to go anywhere she wanted.

But she must never know what he was doing. She must never be permitted to guess that he was deliberately lagging and procrastinating in the construction of the dam and ditches. More than anything else she must never know he was involved in murder. He knew her well enough to be sure that if she ever found out, he would lose her forever, and that was something he could not stand.

CHAPTER SIX

After leaving Judge Porter's office, Brady rode his dust-caked horse back to the courthouse, where Spain's mount stood at the tie rail. He untied the animal without dismounting, then led him down the street to the livery stable.

He was edgy and cross. He rode into the cool shadows of the livery barn and

47

dismounted. Jake Homsher, the liveryman, limped out of a back stall and took the reins.

Brady motioned toward Spain's horse. 'This one of yours?'

Homsher nodded.

'How'd Spain get him?'

Homsher looked at him defiantly. 'How the hell should I know?'

'Was he stolen?'

'Stolen, borrowed—I don't inventory this place every day, and I don't know who took him. I don't even know when he was taken.'

'So you wouldn't have any notion about how Spain got this horse?'

Homsher shook his head, his expression surly.

'Jake, do you know what the penalty is for withholding evidence in a murder case?'

'Don't talk to me about penalties,' Homsher said. 'There ought to be a penalty for bringing a man like Spain in alive. If you'd done what you should—'

Brady, in disgust, turned and walked out of the stable into the street. The sun was setting now. Coolness flowed along the street, touching Brady's sweaty face, and making him think of Shirley Ord.

He wanted to see her, but hated to go to her smelling like a billy goat. He hesitated before the livery barn for a moment, listening to the evening sounds of the town. Then, deciding he was too tired to clean up, he swung abruptly

48

and headed toward the Ord house, hoping that she'd gone home from the store. If she hadn't, he wouldn't see her this evening—he wasn't going to face her brother and a store full of disapproving townspeople to find her.

The Ord house was small, a four-room cottage with a hip-roof and gingerbread scrollwork around the eaves. It had a neat, green yard edged with beds of blue delphiniums, peonies and Shasta daisies. Lilac bushes hid the porch from the house next door.

Brady climbed the sagging steps, thinking that it would take only a few minutes of Pete's time to fix them, but he was an obstinate man with a one-track mind that was fastened on his business. Suddenly Brady smelled frying steak. He didn't knock, but Shirley must have seen him coming. She rushed out, letting the screen door slam behind her.

Shirley was a small girl. The top of her head came to a point on Brady's chest a couple of inches below his jutting chin. Her face was piquant, freckled across the nose, and perhaps not smooth enough to be called really beautiful. Yet she was attractive, perhaps because there was warmth, a bright fire, a womanliness that said this girl had much to give a man she accepted as her own.

A hesitant smile touched her full mouth as she saw him. 'Oh Brady, you look awful.'

He grinned. 'I feel awful, too.'

She crossed the porch to him, and, reaching

up, put her cool hands on the back of his head. Standing on her tiptoes, she pulled his head down and kissed him on the lips.

His arms went around her and pulled her roughly against him. The kiss lengthened until she finally drew back, laughing. 'I guess you're not so tired after all.'

He let her go and, leaning against the porch pillar, grinned at her. 'Aren't you going to ask me to eat?'

'Of course, Brady. Go wash up. I'll set it on the table. We won't wait on Pete. He gets to talking and forgets all about supper.'

Brady followed her through the house that was steamy with the retained heat of the blistering day and the fire Shirley had in the big range. He went through the kitchen and out onto the back porch. He worked the pump handle and filled a washpan with cold water. He washed noisily, making sounds like a boy blowing bubbles, and all the time he was thinking that he knew exactly what Pete Ord was talking about. Tonight Brady Royal and Lee Spain would be the stuff of everybody's gossip in Bear Dance.

Shirley watched him closely. When Brady finished washing and looked up, she tossed him a towel. Drying, he followed her into the kitchen and sat down gratefully at the table. He hung the towel over the back of his chair.

Looking at her, he asked, 'Do you approve or not?'

'Of what?'

'Of the way I brought Spain in. Everyone else thinks I should have killed him and saved the county the expense of a trial.'

'That's a silly question and you know it. Of course I approve.'

'I'm glad somebody does.'

'You shouldn't worry about what people say. It was a terrible crime Lee Spain committed, killing a woman and child. You can't blame people for feeling strongly about it.'

'I don't blame them for feeling strongly,' he said. 'I guess I've got more reason to want him dead than anyone else. But I can blame people for not knowing what they want. First they cuss me because I use my gun too much, and the next thing I know they're on my back because I bring a prisoner in alive.'

Shirley smiled. 'People aren't consistent, Brady. You know that.'

'I guess I do. I can overlook what other people say, but I want you to approve.' He saw her brow furrow and asked, 'What are you thinking now?'

Her smile faded. 'Brady, you know what I think.'

'I couldn't guarantee that I'd live forever even if I resigned tonight,' he said. 'I might cut my throat in the morning when I shave.'

'Oh, be sensible. It isn't the danger that worries me as much as what the job does to you. Being a law officer hardens a man. It makes him bitter because he constantly sees the vicious and sordid side of life. Every time he kills a man, it takes a little more decency out of him. I don't want a husband who will be a different kind of man ten years from now.'

Brady ate ravenously, not saying anything. He tried to stifle a rising irritability, but he wasn't entirely successful. He felt she owed him a little more understanding than she was showing. She had heard the criticisms that had been made of him, and she knew his side of the argument. She knew, too, that he had come around to her way of thinking that the law should be permitted to do its work, and yet she still didn't really understand him. She wanted to change him, and that, he guessed, was what all women wanted to do when they married a man. He didn't think she was really worried so much about what he was going to be. She just didn't like the way he was right now.

'Well,' he said, 'somebody's got to work at the job I'm trying to do.'

'I know,' she agreed. 'I guess it's just that I don't want it to be my man. What I don't like is the sort of thing you have to do. Sitting in the jail sometimes for hours at a time. Getting mixed up in family squabbles. Having to arrest drunks and fight men like Spain.' She shook her head. 'How rewarding a life is it? They use you and throw you away when you're used up. Like Frank Bowie. An old man at fifty-five.

52

What can he do when he finishes his term?'

Brady leaned back in his chair and rolled a cigarette. She was partly right. But she wanted him to go into the store with her brother Pete, and that was something he could never do.

'I can't tie an apron around me and be a counter jumper,' he said.

'I know,' she said. 'I shouldn't have asked you to do that. But there must be something else you can do.'

'I want a ranch some day,' he said. 'Trouble is I haven't saved much money. May be a long time before I have enough.'

He got up from the table, feeling more bitter than he wanted her to know. The men he had killed since he'd put on the star had forced him to kill them, or, in the case of the horse thief, it had been an accident which wouldn't have happened if the man hadn't made a run for it. Those killings hadn't changed him, and he wouldn't be changed by any that might still come. He started toward the door.

'Brady.'

He turned on her and in spite of himself, the angry words came. 'Whatever change has come in me has been for the good. You've helped me believe something that's important. I wanted to kill Spain more than I ever wanted to kill a man in my life, but I didn't and, damn it, you know why.'

A small smile appeared at the corners of

Shirley's mouth. He stopped. Suddenly he grinned and, reaching out, pulled her to him. He put his mouth on hers and found her lips warm and eager. This was the way it had always been after a quarrel. She would come to him as she did now, loving him and wanting him to know it.

Drawing away at last, he said, grinning, 'You sure know how to make a man forget he's tired.'

She put a hand to her head to smooth her hair down. 'Go on now,' she said, pleased. 'Take a bath and go to bed. Next time you come to see me, don't be so cranky.'

He crossed the kitchen and she followed him to the front door. Her brother Pete was coming up the walk. He began to scowl the instant he saw Brady.

'Of all the damn fool things to do,' Pete said angrily. 'Why didn't you feed Spain to the coyotes? A rotten killer like that don't deserve to live.'

Brady felt his hands close into fists as he wondered why a girl like Shirley had to have a bullheaded, sometimes stupid, brother like Pete Ord. Of all the voices that had criticized Brady for being too free with his gun and ignoring legal procedure, Pete's had been the loudest. Now he would be just as loud attacking Brady for not using his gun.

'He hasn't been convicted,' Brady said, trying to keep his temper under control. 'He

54

hasn't even come to trial. I'm not the judge and jury, Pete. Remember?'

'There ain't no doubt about his guilt,' Pete said, his face red. 'What're you trying to do, take Spain's part?'

Brady stared at Pete, at the fat face with the hammering pulse in the temples, and he knew he had to get out of here or he'd smash a fist into the storekeeper's face. Nodding brusquely at Shirley, he stepped around Pete, strode down the walk and into the street without looking back.

He was angry, angry at Shirley for not understanding him, for arguing about what his job would do to him, for not realizing that he would be the worst kind of coward if he quit the job Frank Bowie had trained him for. Worst of all was the obvious fact that she couldn't see he had changed. It had seemed to him that bringing Lee Spain in alive should prove it to anyone.

But it was Pete's talent for switching sides that got under Brady's hide more than Shirley's lack of understanding. Principle meant nothing to Pete Ord, and although this seemed to prove what Frank Bowie had said many times about voters and what any man who held public office had to put up with, it didn't make Brady feel any better.

He walked into the hotel, picked up his key at the desk, and slogged up the stairs. He stripped to his underwear and flopped in exhaustion on the bed. There was a short moment before he went to sleep, and in that moment he thought of Isaac Porter. He remembered Porter's eyes, the ruthless eyes of a man who, once started down the road he had chosen, would stay on that road until the very end.

He would have another talk with Porter in the morning. Maybe he'd ask Bowie to hire a second deputy to help guard Spain. In the morning he'd . . . Then he stopped thinking. The exhaustion of the chase, of the sleepless nights was too much, and he fell into a sleep that was very much like death.

CHAPTER SEVEN

Isaac Porter was tense and worried as he closed his front gate and went up the walk to his house. He felt as though he were waiting for a bomb to explode. Actually that was just about the way another jail break would affect the town.

He hoped there would be no trouble about it, but he had little faith in Dude Vedder. After Courtney had mentioned the boy, Porter remembered seeing him around town. Porter was fairly familiar with his breed. Vedder was a cheap braggart without the tough courage of Lee Spain, and without the ability to use his head under the pressure of danger. He might, coming up against an old, steady hand like Sheriff Bowie, get himself killed.

Well, if that happened, Porter would have to put the job on the shoulders of Courtney and Lund. At least he could trust them to get it done. Again he thought he should have used them instead of Spain in the first place. Still, he had hated to risk them, and still did. He might need them later.

He closed the door wearily behind him, suddenly conscious of his age, of the tiredness that was an ache in his body.

Marian looked up from a chair and laid her book aside. She smiled at him, but it was a tight, uneasy smile.

She was like all young people, Porter thought. He should have foreseen this when he married her. She had no patience. If she wanted something, she had to have it right now. She wanted to live in the city where there was gaiety—parties and excitement. And she'd live there, too, but she'd have to wait a couple of years at least. She'd have to wait until Porter's business was finished in Bear Dance. He hadn't told her so, though. He was afraid to.

'You look tired, dear,' she said. 'Did you have a hard day?'

He shook his head, smiling. 'It's just the heat, I guess. And that business of Spain being brought in. He sent for me, you know. Wanted me to represent him.'

'You're not going to?'

'Of course not. He killed some of my people.'

He thought a strange expression crossed her face as he said, 'my people.' He asked, 'How was your day?' and bent to kiss her lips, but she turned her head quickly so that his lips touched her cheek.

'All right, I suppose,' she said. 'Just as deadly as every day has been lately.' She rose and faced him. 'I can't stand this place any longer, Ike. I wish you'd send me to Denver. Or San Francisco. Just a short trip so I can get my breath and escape for a few days from this stupid little town.'

He turned his back and, walking to the window, stared out into the street. He was afraid, as terribly afraid as he had ever been in his life. The town was pretty awful, but he couldn't risk sending her away. She was young, only twenty-four, and he was fifty-five. If she were away, he'd wonder constantly whom she was with, what she was doing. He hadn't succeeded in making her happy. And if she were away she'd perhaps justify indiscretions with the memory of that unhappiness with him.

He certainly couldn't leave now, and he couldn't let her go alone. But if he didn't take her on a trip, he thought in panic, anything could happen. She might even run away.

Turning, he forced a tolerant smile to his lips. 'You're right, my dear. We both need a trip. Give me a couple of weeks to set things straight, then we'll go away.

Her face brightened immediately, and he could almost see her thoughts. Suddenly a feeling of tenderness for her overcame him. If only he were twenty years younger . . .

She'd married him for security and position, he knew, and he'd given her little of either until he'd come here. Actually, he had first thought of this irrigation scheme under pressure from Marian and her obvious need for luxury he had not been able to afford. He'd known he was losing her, known he had to make money, a lot of it and fast.

Yet even now in this house and with all the money she needed to spend, she wasn't satisfied. He wondered if she would ever be satisfied—even in a city—even with all the money she could use there. Perhaps her discontent had a deeper root. Perhaps, now that there had been time to consider her bargain, she regretted marrying a man thirty years older than she was.

The thought was bitter. Damn it, he'd been an honest man before he'd married her. Well, comparatively honest. At least he'd never done anything that was actually illegal. Now he was involved in murder—the most sordid and brutal kind of murder possible, that of a woman and child. And it wasn't his fault, either. Damn it, if Spain had only used his head . . .

He caught himself listening for gunshots, and scoffed inwardly at his nervousness. Hell, he wouldn't hear anything this far away, particularly if the sound was muffled by the courthouse walls.

Marian came to him, put her arms around him, and laid her head against his chest. She looked up in her consciously childlike way, and asked coaxingly, 'Couldn't we go tomorrow? Couldn't your old business wait?'

He looked at her, really seeing her for the first time. Right now she was like a child trying to wheedle a father into agreeing to something he had said he couldn't do. And he thought bitterly, If I say yes, she'll reward me suitably in our bedroom tonight.

He disengaged her arms and stepped away. 'No, we can't. Damn it, aren't you ever satisfied? You want a trip. All right, we'll take a trip, but by God, you can wait two weeks.'

She stood staring at him like a petulant child. Suddenly his anger boiled to the surface. He thought he'd married a woman. She was old enough to be a woman. It was time she began acting like one.

'I'm in a jam around here,' he said harshly, 'whether you know it or not. People are beginning to say I don't intend to build the dam. I can't just up and leave at a time—'

'*Do* you intend to build the dam?'

60

'Of course I do.'

'Then why do they say you don't? Why has it taken you so long?'

'Because I want it to. You don't think for a minute I can make any money on the project if I finish it this summer, do you? It'll take years. With what I got out of this bunch of settlers I can barely pay off the land, pay salaries to the men I need, and live through the year the way you think you have to live.'

He thought her face turned a shade paler, but he wasn't sure. Sometimes he wondered if she understood anything except such subjects as a trip or a new dress or another piece of jewelry. Still, she had a strange code of ethics that was strict and almost as childish as some of her other reactions.

'Exactly what do you plan to do?' she asked coldly.

He should have been warned by the tone of her voice, but he was too angry to notice. 'I intend to stall. Maybe for a couple more years. The settlers who are on the land now won't be able to meet their notes in the fall unless they have a crop and they sure can't get one this year. The land will come back to me, and I'll sell it again next year, and the year after that. Then I'll build the dam. And when I do, people will forget about the ones who went broke. They'll only think of the ones who succeeded. I'll be a big man in this country and a rich one. There'll be no limit to where I can go and you'll go with me.'

'Ike,' she said, 'that's dishonest.'

'Of course it's dishonest. And why do you suppose I'm doing it? For you, that's why. I'm doing it because you're always so damned dissatisfied.'

'Don't blame your actions on me,' she said in a small, even voice.

'I'll put the blame where it belongs. And I'll tell you something else.'

'There's more?'

He turned and walked away from her. He'd come close to telling her the whole story, about hiring Spain and all that had resulted from it, but this would have been a really bad mistake. She could bend her moral standards to a point, but no further, just as she had before they were married. He didn't pretend to understand it. He only knew that was the way she was.

Eventually she would get used to the idea of cheating a bunch of settlers out of their savings, but she would never get used to the idea of murder. He had never seen her as completely outraged as when she'd heard of the murder of Mrs. Van Schoen and her boy. The way Porter saw it, this was part of Marian's childishness. If you're dishonest to a point, you find yourself in time reaching for a place where you can't draw a line, but he could talk for a week without making Marian understand it.

He turned back to face her. 'There's more, all right, but not the way you think. You married me, knowing how old I was. You went into it with your eyes open. Why? I've often asked myself that question. I suppose the answer is a simple one. You wanted the things I could give you.'

'The things I *thought* you could give me,' she said.

He stared at her. Well, she was mature enough when she gave him an answer like that. And honest. Too damn honest. God, sometimes he wanted to wring her pretty neck. And if he stayed here, he might do it.

He turned and went out the door, calling back, 'I'll get supper downtown.'

That had been close back there. He couldn't afford any more fits of temper like that no matter how much Marian angered him. If he had admitted complicity in the Van Schoen murders to her, she would have walked out immediately. Probably would have gone to Sheriff Bowie, or Brady Royal.

Porter moved down the walk to the gate, opened it, and started downtown, a feeling of depression beginning to weigh upon him. What did he have, really, for all his scheming? He couldn't count on the loyalty of his wife. He had no close friends. The settlers out on the flat distrusted him. The people in town showed respect, even fear, but now that the settlers' money had run out . . .

Next year it would be different, of course. He'd have a new bunch of settlers on the land. They'd be buying things in town, and folks would praise him again for bringing prosperity to Bear Dance.

If there was a next year for him. If Vedder didn't bungle the job of breaking Spain out of jail. If Royal didn't catch Jim and bring him back as he had before . . .

He stopped and stared along the street, and suddenly realized he couldn't go down there. He must be at home when the commotion broke. He couldn't afford to do anything that Brady could call unusual.

Turning, he retraced his steps to the house. He went in by a side door that led to his study, got a bottle out of a desk drawer and poured himself a drink. He gulped it and poured another, hearing his wife moving about in the kitchen as she prepared her supper.

Porter was hungry, tired, irritable and depressed. He was a big man. He'd be bigger before he was through, a hell of a lot bigger. Why, then, did he have to feel like such a failure?

Quickly, because he could not face the answer to that question, he took another drink.

CHAPTER EIGHT

Lee Spain was awake. The jail was quiet. So was the town. The only sound Spain heard was the cry of a night bird hunting along the creek, a raucous, lonely cry that came to him faintly through the barred, open window.

By listening carefully, Spain could hear the sheriff's snores from the office, and occasionally the creaking of the cot in there as Bowie shifted his position. The pale light of a single coal-oil lamp came through the open door and made a square pattern on the floor of the jail corridor.

Carefully, so as to make no noise, Spain sat up on his cot. In spite of this caution, the springs creaked. He froze, wondering at this stealth in himself, wondering at the tautness of his nerves and muscles.

But he knew—he wasn't sure how he knew but he knew—something was going to happen within minutes. And he had to be ready when it did.

Fear was a brief coldness in him as he considered the possibility that a lynch mob might even now be creeping along the courthouse hall, hoping to take the sheriff by surprise. Spain opened his mouth to shout, then shut it abruptly, making no sound. Because more likely it wasn't a lynch mob.

More likely it was the man Porter had sent to break him out.

Spain eased himself carefully off the cot and, sitting on the floor, pulled on his boots. He got up and tiptoed across the cell to the window, which he could look through by standing on his toes.

From the position of the moon, he judged that the hour must be three or a little after. It would be getting light soon. There wasn't much time.

Quietly, he crossed the cell again and stopped at the bars next to the corridor. He listened intently, but heard nothing except Sheriff Bowie's soft snores.

Suddenly he heard the sheriff's cot creak loudly. He heard a wordless exclamation from Bowie, then immediately there was the sodden sound of gun barrel striking flesh and bone. The sound was unmistakable, like the thud of a cleaver biting through rib bones on a butcher's block.

Spain's breath sighed out in relief. Quick and efficient. Bowie would be out cold from that blow.

He waited. Then he heard the sound again. And again. Now, with each blow, someone grunted from exertion.

It was eerie listening, because Spain knew he was hearing Bowie die, hearing a savage murder, senseless and without point. Bowie was no danger to Spain. He couldn't ride. All that was necessary was to knock him out.

Spain felt a quick burst of anger that grew into quiet fury. It had nothing to do with the sheriff's death. Spain had killed many times, in his life—for money—in self-defense—to avoid exposure for other crimes he had committed, but he had never killed senselessly and without purpose. The way he saw it, only a stupid man made things tougher for himself by killing needlessly.

The sounds in the office changed. There was still the creaking of the cot, still the sodden sounds of blows. But the grunts of exertion had changed into a continuous sound of sobbing exhaustion. Spain wanted to shout at whoever it was to stop and come let him out. But he didn't dare. The window was open. Someone out in the street might hear.

So he waited. At last the blows stopped and a man came through the door into the jail corridor. A chill raced down Spain's spine. The newcomer held a gun in his hand. The gun was red with blood, and blood had splattered like polka dots over the man's face and shirt front. There was wildness in the stranger's eyes, an expression Spain had never seen in a man's eyes before.

Spain said harshly, breaking the spell that was on him, 'Damn it, you took long enough for that. Brady Royal was beat when he brought me in or he'd never have gone home and left the sheriff alone. But he ain't going to

67

sleep forever. So get a move on. Open that door and give me a gun.'

Now he saw that the stranger was only a boy, eighteen or nineteen. His face was bright with sweat, and his hand trembled as he clumsily inserted the key in the lock.

Spain pushed the door open and stepped into the corridor. He walked toward the office and went inside. After one quick glance at Frank Bowie's body, he didn't look again. Instead, he stared at the boy. This one was crazy. You'd have to be crazy to go on beating a thing like that on the cot.

For an instant awe combined with disgust in Spain. Then he crossed the room, selected a rifle from the rack and took his own gun and belt from the peg on which it hung. He went through the sheriff's desk drawers until he found one that was filled with ammunition. He selected a box of cartridges that fitted the rifle he'd picked and stuffed it into his pocket.

He looked at the stranger again. 'Who the hell are you?'

'Dude Vedder.' The strange intensity had gone from Vedder's eyes. Now he looked pale and exhausted.

'His honor sure picked a stupid one to break me out,' Spain said tonelessly. 'You didn't have to kill the sheriff. Now they'll be a hundred times more anxious to catch up with us. And if they do, it won't be a trial we'll get. It'll be a noose before we can catch our breath.'

68

Vedder didn't say anything. He just stood there staring vacantly at Spain.

Again Spain felt disgust. 'Come on, damn it,' he said as he strapped on his gun bolt. 'It'll be light soon.'

They walked quietly out of the courthouse. In the east there was a thin line of gray that lay like smoke along the horizon. Spain thought about the sheriff lying on the cot in his office, and what would happen to Brady Royal when he found the body. He'd go crazy. This time Royal wouldn't aim to bring him in alive.

There had to be some way . . . A hostage! That was it. Someone Royal thought a lot of. Someone whose safety meant more to him than revenge for Bowie's death. That girl . . . what was her name? Ord. Shirley Ord. That was it.

Spain looked at Vedder. 'You know where the storekeeper lives? Ord?'

'Sure. I've had my eyes on his sister. Followed her home once.'

'All right. Where'd you leave the horses?'

'Back there,' Vedder said. 'Behind the courthouse.'

Spain ran across the parched lawn, hearing the grass rustle beneath his feet. The gray in the east was stronger now.

Two saddle horses stood behind the courthouse, idly munching dry grass. Spain caught one of them, picking the one that looked freshest, and swung to the saddle.

Vedder, panting from the run, mounted the other.

'Get another horse with a sidesaddle,' Spain said. 'Bring it to the Ord house.'

'Now wait a minute,' Vedder said angrily. 'Who do you think you're giving orders to?'

'I know who I'm giving orders to. A stupid kid who beat the sheriff to death when he didn't have to. Now do as I say or draw your gun.'

Vedder didn't move, but even in the darkness Spain could feel the boy's hate. And in that instant he knew he'd have to kill Vedder before he was through. Not tonight, though. Not here in town. He was in a tight enough spot now. No sense making it worse.

Vedder finally stepped into the saddle and rode away for the third horse. Spain mounted, sat motionless for a moment as he listened, then hearing nothing that seemed unusual he rode to the Ord house, tied his horse, and moved silently across the lawn.

He tried the door knob, and the door opened easily. He stepped into the house, waited a moment until he could see again, then crossed the room to a door. It opened into the dining room. Another door opened into a hall. Spain eased himself through the door and down the hall, gun in hand.

The first room he entered was Pete Ord's, who was snoring lustily. Spain crossed to him and clipped him, hard, just above the ear with the gun barrel. Pete's snoring stopped abruptly.

Spain left the room and entered the one at the other end of the hall. He could make out the form of a woman on the bed. The covers were thrown back against the heat of the night, and the moon, shining in the window, outlined her bare shoulders and partly bare breasts.

As he crossed to the bed, a board squeaked under his foot. Shirley Ord sat up. Spain lunged at her and falling on top of her, forced her shoulders back against the bed. He groped for her mouth, found it, and clamped a hand over it. Shirley bit his hand savagely, struggling and scratching and kicking, but failing to free herself.

Spain yanked his hand away and, before she could scream, jammed his gun against her head. He said, 'I don't want to hurt you, but you've got to be quiet. I'll kill you if you don't.'

He could feel her nearly naked body trembling beneath him, but realized there'd be time enough for that later when he was safely away from town.

She said in a small, tight voice, 'What do you want?'

'I've got to have a hostage to keep Royal off my trail, and you're it. Get up and dress.

She didn't reply, and he took her silence for agreement. He got up and stepped back.

'You'll have to leave the room.'

Spain grinned. 'Nothin' doin, girlie. I've felt

71

everything you've got anyway. Won't hurt you none for me to see it.'

She grabbed up the lamp from the bedside table and threw it at him. He ducked, and it smashed against the wall. The fumes of coal oil filled the room.

Spain chuckled. 'A regular little she-cat, ain't you? Well, just keep it up and I'll kill you and your brother both.' He glanced nervously at the window. The sky was gray.

He lowered his voice. 'I'm playing for keeps, girlie. I can't be any worse off than I am now no matter what else I do. You've got two minutes to get dressed. When the two minutes are up, you're dead if you're not ready. That plain?'

'What have you done to Pete?'

'Slugged him. Before I leave, I'll tie him up if you behave. If you don't, I'll finish him now.'

She turned her back and let the nightgown slide to the floor. Spain drew a sharp breath. This girl was a real beauty. He grinned, thinking ahead to the long nights on the trail.

She dressed hastily and turned when she finished. Spain said, 'Now go on down the hall to your brother's room.'

She obeyed, Spain following. He rolled Pete off the bed and began to tear the sheets into strips. Shirley knelt and laid her head against Pete's chest. Then she snatched the remainder of the sheet from Spain and bandaged Pete's head while Spain tied his feet.

With that done, Spain rolled Pete on his face and tied his hands behind him. Shirley put the pillow under Pete's head.

'All right,' Spain said. 'Get outside. Yell once and I'll kill you and come back and kill Pete too. Understand?'

She nodded. She walked through the house and went out into the front yard. Vedder waited, his mount standing beside Spain's horse. He had a third animal with a sidesaddle on his back.

Spain took a cartridge from his belt. With its lead end he scrawled on the top board of the white picket gate: *Trail me and your sister dies. Spain.*

He shoved the cartridge back into a loop and mounted. Shirley was already up. 'Come on,' he said, and rode south into the graying dawn.

CHAPTER NINE

Brady was awakened by a heavy pounding on his door. He had scarcely opened his eyes when Pete Ord burst into the room. Dazed and startled, Brady swung his legs over the side of the bed. Pete's face was beaded with sweat, reddened by exertion and fury, but it was his eyes that caught and held Brady's attention. They were scared eyes, the eyes of a man who was almost crazy.

Pete's mouth worked, but no words came. His breath whistled in and out of his heaving lungs. Brady reached for his pants and pulled them on hurriedly. He said, 'All right, Pete. Sit down. When you get your breath, tell me about it.'

But he knew, or thought he did, what Pete wanted to tell him. Spain had broken jail again.

Pete didn't sit down. He glared at Brady, then burst out, 'Spain broke jail.' He swallowed, fought for breath, and then got the rest of it out. 'He's got Shirley. Damn it, do something.'

Brady yanked on his boots, then straightened and seized his shirt. He crammed on his hat, buckled gun and belt around his lean hips, and burst from the room, still tucking his shirt tail into his pants.

He took the stairs at a dead run, with Pete Ord close at his heels. He angled across the street, still running. He raced up the courthouse steps, barely hearing Pete's yell, 'What're you going in there for? Damn it, I told you Spain had Shirley with him.'

Brady ran along the hall, the disinfectant smell of the jail strong in his nostrils. His brain was nearly frozen with fear, fear for Frank Bowie, who had been on guard last night and who should have been the one to give the alarm.

He skidded as he turned the corner into the sheriff's office, recovered, and came to an abrupt, shocked halt just inside the door.

Frank Bowie lay on his cot against the wall. There was nothing about him that was recognizable except his clothes. His face was a horror that Brady would never forget as long as he lived.

Blood drenched the upper part of the cot, the pillow, the floor beneath it. It was even spattered on the wall, as it often is in a slaughterhouse.

Pete came in behind Brady, looked, then turned and ran into the hall. Brady heard him vomiting out there. The retching sounds diminished until the courthouse door slammed shut, then silence.

For a long time shock held Brady. Then something else began taking over—an implacable fury that would grow and grow until it consumed him. Or until Spain was dead.

Bowie had been right. They had all been right. He should have killed Spain out there in the mountains when he'd had a chance.

He hadn't taken his eyes from Bowie's still, twisted form. Now, as he stood there, a new thought crept into his mind. Spain hadn't done this. Spain was a killer, a bad one, but not a senseless killer. He was a saint by comparison to the one who had done this.

No, Spain hadn't done it. He might have

killed the sheriff during his escape, but he wouldn't have hammered Bowie's face to a pulp. He wouldn't have stood there, straddling Bowie's body, beating, pounding on something that was already dead.

Someone else had to have helped Spain escape. And this had to be that other man's work.

Brady walked along the hall and out into the pleasant morning air. Pete Ord sat on the steps, his head hanging between his knees. His face, turned shiny by a film of sweat, was an unhealthy green color. As Brady sat down beside him, Pete groaned, 'It's awful. I never saw anything like it before.'

'What happened last night?' Brady said.

'I don't know. I woke up about dawn with my head splitting wide open. I was on the floor and tied with strips torn off the sheets. I had a lump on my head above my right ear. I guess it took me most of an hour to get loose. Then I found out Shirley was gone.'

Brady didn't speak. After a moment Pete added, 'I found a note scrawled on the fence with a bullet. It said, "Trail me and your sister dies." It was signed, "Spain."'

So Spain had Shirley. That was bad enough. But with Spain, undoubtedly, was the crazed killer who had beaten Bowie to death, who had even beaten him after he was dead. A man capable of that was capable of anything.

Brady rose, went back into the courthouse

76

and selected a rifle from the rack, not looking at Bowie's body. He crossed the room to the desk, opened a drawer, and took out a couple of boxes of cartridges for the rifle. Then he left the room.

Outside in the hall he met the courthouse janitor, Luke, coming in through the front door with one of the restaurant trays. Brady stopped him and took the tray from him. 'Get Doc, Luke—the sheriff's dead and Spain's gone.'

Luke stared at him, then turned and hurried outside and down the stairs. Brady took the tray with him and set it down at the top of the steps. Even the thought of food nauseated him, but he knew he needed the strength it would give him.

'Come and eat, Pete,' Brady said. 'You'll feel better.'

Pete looked at him incredulously. He shook his head. Brady uncovered the tray. He poured and gulped a cup of steaming black coffee. Then he began to choke down the food on one of the plates. His stomach rebelled, but he kept on.

'What are you going to do?' Pete asked.

'Go after them. What else is there to do?'

'You can't. He said he'd kill her.'

'What do you want me to do, sit here on my butt and hope he turns her loose alive? If I don't get to her in time, she might be better off if he does kill her.'

'I don't know.' Pete put a hand to his aching head. 'I can't think. Oh, my God, I don't know.'

Down the street Brady saw Luke returning with the doctor, a crowd of eight or ten men dogging their heels. The doctor and Luke went on into the courthouse, but Brady stopped the others. 'Stay out of there. It's nothing any of you want to see.'

A man in the crowd muttered, 'This wouldn't have happened if you'd taken care of Spain when you had the chance.'

Brady didn't answer. He didn't feel like arguing, or even defending himself. He rose and went down the steps, saw Courtney and Lund in the crowd, and briefly wondered if either of them were capable of the savage act that had taken place last night. He decided they weren't. They were hardcases, and doubtless wouldn't hesitate over a killing, but they wouldn't do it that way.

His mind searched around, trying to decide who, of the men he knew in the Sundown Creek country, was capable of murdering a man as Frank Bowie had been murdered. The only name that came into his mind was Dude Vedder.

As he pushed through the crowd, a man said, 'Swear us in, Royal. Let's go get him.'

Brady shook his head. 'He's got Shirley Ord. If a posse goes after him, no telling what he'll do. I'll have to go alone.'

He strode on down the street to the livery barn. The liveryman, Jake Homsher, hadn't got there yet, so he caught and saddled his own horse. He mounted and started toward the store, then remembered it was closed, that Pete Ord was still at the courthouse.

He rode past the store to the restaurant and there bought the supplies he needed: a side of bacon, a five-pound sack of coffee, flour, and a few other items he knew he would need. The few in front of the courthouse had grown to an angry, muttering crowd.

Brady tied the sack of supplies behind his saddle. Looking up, he saw Pete Ord hurrying toward him. He waited, and when Pete reached him, he said, 'Brady, you're a damn fool. He'll kill her if he knows you're following 'em. You're not going. I won't let you in.'

'You can't stop me,' Brady said.

'The hell I can't.'

Brady stared at Pete's face a long moment. Pete Ord was invariably loud in his opinions, as changeable as the spring wind, and always certain he was right. But how he could fail to understand what lay ahead for Shirley was beyond Brady's understanding.

'If I can't get to her in time,' Brady said, 'I hope Spain does kill her. You saw Bowie's body. Spain didn't do it. Someone else did, someone who's more animal than human. You want to leave Shirley with someone like that?'

Brady's words only seemed to confuse Pete.

He slumped against the hitchrail in front of the restaurant, his eyes glazed. 'I don't know. God, I just don't know.'

'I do, Pete. Believe me, I do. I love her too much to let her stay with that pair.'

He swung into the saddle, reined his horse around, and rode out of town. He doubted if Spain would be fool enough to try to confuse him this time. The outlaw would be interested only in speed.

Brady headed south, convinced that Spain would try for the Colorado line. Brady couldn't legally follow him there, because he had no authority outside Wyoming. Spain would know, of course, that a barrier such as a state line wouldn't stop Brady, but he'd want to take advantage of everything he could, and from past experience Brady knew that it was sometimes possible for a fugitive to set one lawman against another, especially when one was invading the province of the second.

Brady rode clear of the town for about a mile, then left the road and began a half circle, looking for tracks. He found them almost at once. He'd been hoping he'd find only two sets of tracks, which would have meant Spain and Shirley had left the killer behind. But there were three sets of tracks, the individual prints fairly far apart, and scuffed. The horses had been running hard.

Brady swung into the trail and lifted his own horse to a lope, keeping his eyes steadily on the ground. Yesterday's weariness was gone in the urgency of the moment. He wondered what time last night Bowie had been killed. He tried to remember how dry the blood had been on Bowie, on the pillow, on the wall. For a time his mind refused to focus on what he had seen, and finally the mental picture came clear—the blood had been red, not brown.

The murder, then, must have happened in the early part of the morning. But even so, Spain had a start of at least two hours, and this time the man would be hard to catch. Spain wouldn't stop. He wouldn't camp. He'd keep on going all day, and all night too, unless he was unable to secure fresh horses or unless Shirley gave out on him. He'd ration out the strength in his horses the way an Apache does, caring nothing about the horses, caring only that they didn't die before reaching a place where others were available.

Brady was two miles or more from town when he heard a distant shout behind him, followed by three quick-triggered pistol shots. Looking back, he saw a single rider coming fast behind him.

He refused to stop, but did haul in on his horse's reins until the animal was traveling at a steady trot. When he glanced back a second time, he recognized Pete Ord and muttered a curse.

He didn't want Pete along. He didn't want anyone along. If he got Shirley safely away from the killers, he'd need all the luck he could get. Pete wouldn't help. He was too likely to go off half-cocked.

It took Pete nearly half an hour to catch up. When he did range alongside Brady's horse, his face was red with anger. 'What's the matter with you?' he shouted. 'Didn't you hear me yell?'

'Yeah, I heard. What'd you want me to do, stop and wait?'

Brady put his horse into a lope, and Pete matched the pace. Brady yelled, 'Go on back. I'll handle this.'

'Like you handled it last night?' When Brady didn't answer, Pete shouted, 'We've got to stay far enough behind 'em so they won't know they're being followed. Otherwise, Shirley will—'

'Shirley's safe enough right now,' Brady interrupted. 'She's their hostage, remember? They won't hurt her today.'

'What do you mean, today?'

'That's what I meant. Today. But if they stop tonight . . .'

'By God, they'd better not—'

'What have they got to lose?'

Pete drove spurs into his horses's sides and the animal broke into a dead run. Brady lunged his horse ahead and seized the headstall of Pete's horse pulling the gelding to a stop.

'You're going back,' Brady said.

'Like hell. I'm going after Shirley.'

Brady slapped his face, a hard blow that rocked the older man's head. 'You're a fool. You always have been. Now go on and tie your apron on and get behind your damn counter. It's all you're fit for. Keep me here arguing with you much longer and I'll never catch up with them in time. Go along and act like you're acting now, and you'll get your sister killed for sure.'

For a moment Pete glared at him, his angry face showing how close his temper was to the breaking point. Brady tensed, expecting Pete to swing on him. Then, with startling suddenness, Pete caved in.

'Please, Brady, let me go. I'll do exactly what you tell me. I've got to go. I've got to help. I'd go wild waiting back in town.' He swallowed, then added, 'I guess Shirley thinks like you do, that I'm not good for anything except wearing an apron behind a counter. This is my chance to show her something different.'

Brady almost pitied Pete. He had never liked the man and he had resented Pete's attitude of critical superiority toward him. But right now he couldn't doubt Pete's sincerity. Also, he understood something he should have understood before, that Pete's loud-mouthed opinions and criticisms were cover-ups for his lack of self-confidence.

Brady hesitated, glancing first along the trail

83

ahead, then back at the town. He didn't want Pete along, because he knew Pete's sudden reasonableness was only temporary. It wasn't in the man to do what he was told if he disagreed. And yet any more delay arguing the point might be more dangerous than having Pete along. Brady felt certain that nothing he could do or say would keep Pete from following him. Only by knocking the man out could he go on without him. Even then Brady couldn't be sure Pete wouldn't follow, and show up when his presence was most dangerous to Brady's plans.

Brady shrugged. 'All right. On one condition. By God, you'll do exactly what I tell you whether you think it's right or wrong. Savvy?'

'All right, Brady.'

Doubtfully Brady swung away and touched spurs lightly to his horse's side.

After that he paced the horse as carefully as he knew Spain was pacing his. There was a roadhouse about fifty miles south of Bear Dance, the first and only place where Spain could obtain a change of horses. Brady had to get there fast, but he also had to get there with his horse under him.

Silently Pete Ord followed. The miles flowed along beneath their horses' hoofs, the day growing hotter as the sun climbed toward the middle of the sky.

Brady could only hope he reached the

roadhouse in time. If he didn't . . . He shivered, knowing he couldn't trail the three in darkness. If they stayed the night at the roadhouse, he'd catch them, but if they were able to change horses, they would undoubtedly go on, gaining a whole night's lead. More than that, Shirley would be at their mercy whenever and wherever they camped. Brady would be stuck at the roadhouse for the night, unable to help her, unable to keep away from her the savage animal that had butchered Frank Bowie.

CHAPTER TEN

Porter woke at dawn, an unusual circumstance for him. Ordinarily, he didn't get up before seven o'clock. Upon awakening, he instantly realized the situation he was in, remembered the steps he had taken, and wondered how the night had gone.

He looked at his wife, gave her a sickly smile and looked quickly away. He swung his bony legs over the side of the bed and groped with his feet for his slippers.

He said, 'Stay in bed, my dear. No need for you to get up yet.'

When she didn't reply, he glanced at her again. There was no doubt about the expression in her eyes. She obviously hated him.

He was suddenly conscious of his skinny legs beneath the hem of his nightshirt, of his rumpled, thinning hair and his gray-whiskered jaws. He felt every year of his age, but his wife, the sheet tucked up under her chin so he saw only her face and hair against the pillow, looked more like a girl than a woman.

Vague anger stirred in him. He turned and left the room, gathering up his clothes as he went.

He dressed in the hall, ashamed and angry with himself for doing so. Damn her, he thought. She had no right to humiliate him, no right to make him feel so sharply the difference in their ages, not after all that he had done for her, and because of her.

He'd been good enough for her when she'd thought he could give her the luxuries she wanted. Hell, when you boiled it down, she was nothing but a high-priced whore. What was marriage anyhow but legalized prostitution for a woman like that? She'd sold herself to him, and she had no right to renege on her bargain now.

He finished dressing and went downstairs, feeling a little better for having brought his wife down from her high and mighty position, if only in his mind.

He went out on the porch back of the kitchen and pumped a basin full of cold water. He washed his face briskly, feeling the tension that was building in him. Damn it, why couldn't Courtney and Lund have brought him word?

He dried, returned to the kitchen and built a fire. He put a tea kettle of water on the front of the range to heat and sat down to wait. After a time he realized the fire wasn't crackling. He got up and lifting one of the front lids, saw that the kindling hadn't caught.

Getting out his knife, he whittled off some more shavings, touched a match to them, and sat down to wait again. For the second time the fire went out. He swore angrily, thinking that here was a good example of how inept he was at anything that required skill with his hands.

He had a good mind, a mind that would have brought him to the top of the pile if he had been willing to sit down as a young man and make the law his career. But he'd always been fiddle-footed, more willing to scheme up some kind of a swindle than to work day after day building up a law practice.

To hell with it. His wife could build the fire. He couldn't sit still, not knowing what had happened. He returned to the porch, pumped another basin of water, and began to shave with it. He hated to have to depend on men like Courtney and Lund—on hard-cases like Lee Spain and Dude Vedder. He had the brains and could plan exactly what they were to do, but too often it didn't work out because of the stupidity of the men he had to work with. Spain killing Van Schoen's wife and boy, for example. Now, to compound the felony, he had agreed to using Dude Vedder to free Spain.

His hands trembled so violently that he cut himself twice before he finished shaving. He dried his face, patting the cuts with the towel until they stopped bleeding, then he knotted his tie, slipped on his coat, and picking up his hat, went out through the front door.

The sun was above the horizon when he hurried downtown. Another clear sky and another hot day. By the time he reached the business block, he saw that a crowd had gathered in front of the courthouse. Instantly elation spread a warm glow through his body. Vedder had been successful. Spain was gone.

He fought an urge to go on down and hear the details. It was unusual enough for him to be abroad this early in the morning without making it look any worse.

He turned into the restaurant, ordered ham and eggs, and watched as Courtney and Lund came in and sat down beside him at the counter.

Porter looked at Courtney questioningly and Courtney gave him a bare, half-inch nod. He said in a conversational tone, 'Heard what happened, Judge?'

'No. Something happen?'

The counterman set Porter's plate in front

of him as Courtney said, 'Sure did. Somebody broke Spain out of jail during the night. Killed Frank Bowie doing it. Then Spain and whoever it was with him grabbed Shirley Ord and left town.'

Porter thought he was going to be sick. Bowie dead! Shirley Ord kidnapped!

Courtney watched him, a half smile tugging at the ends of his thick lips. He said deliberately, 'I hear Pete Ord took one look at Bowie's body and heaved his guts all over the courthouse hall. I never figured Pete had a weak stomach, so Bowie must've looked pretty bad. Pete said Bowie was beat to death. Said his face looked like a . . .'

Porter fought against nausea for a moment, conquered it, and fumbled for a cigar. When he had it going, he composed his features and paid his bill.

Courtney and Lund were frankly amused. They might as well have said in words what they were thinking: If you haven't got the stomach for murder, you shouldn't have got mixed up in it.

Porter said, 'I suppose Royal is getting up a posse.'

'Not him,' Courtney said, chuckling. 'He figures he's a one-man army. Started out alone. Spain left a note on the fence at Ord's house sayin' he'd kill Shirley if he was followed.'

Porter muttered, 'He will, too.'

Courtney nodded, then said, 'Royal caught him once, but I wouldn't bet he'll do it this time.'

Again Porter felt the clutching weakness of panic. If Brady Royal did catch Spain . . . if he brought Spain back . . . Spain might talk. Or if Spain didn't Dude Vedder would. Spain had a code of sorts, but Vedder didn't. And he'd crack under pressure.

Porter glanced at Courtney, knowing he had to have time to think this out. He said briskly, 'Come over to my office after a while. I want to talk to you. And don't be all day about it, either.'

He left the restaurant and went into the street, pausing there a moment as he glanced toward the courthouse. The crowd was breaking up. Porter saw the doctor come out, carrying his small black bag. The Van Schoen murders, then this. Frank Bowie had been sheriff a long time, and he'd been criticized just as any man was who carried the star, but he'd been well liked and respected, too. The way he'd been killed would add to the indignation of the public. Damn that Dude Vedder. He wasn't just stupid. He was an idiot.

Porter turned toward his office, keeping the mask of benign good will upon his face. A couple of settlers who had just driven into town glared at him from inside their wagon. He nodded to them affably as he said, 'Good morning.' They didn't reply.

He passed several townsmen on the way to his office. To one he said, 'Terrible thing. Terrible.' The man looked at him doubtfully, nodded, and went on down the street.

Damn it, people seemed to be turning against him. If anything more like this happened . . . or if Spain and Vedder were returned to trial . . . He couldn't afford to let anything else happen. He'd be finished for good if it did.

He climbed the steps to his office wearily, not yet sure what he would do. If he could have had Courtney or Lund shoot Spain while he was in jail, everything would have been fine. Spain's mouth would have been shut for good, Vedder wouldn't have been brought into the thing, and Frank Bowie would he alive. But Spain had taken insurance against that happening by sending a statement to someone in Cheyenne . . . And suddenly he knew he had been as stupid as Lee Spain, or Vedder.

He had half suspected that Spain might be lying about sending that statement to a friend in Cheyenne. Now he realized he should have known absolutely that Spain was lying. The reason was simple—Spain would never put himself so completely in the hands of another man, friend or not. Professionals like Spain knew that they could trust no one.

Very well, then. He must protect himself. Spain must not return. Nor must Vedder. He knew exactly what must be done, and this time he'd leave it to Courtney and Lund, who wouldn't botch the job. It was fortunate that Brady Royal had gone out alone. If he'd taken a posse, what Porter had in mind would have been impossible.

Presently he heard the heavy tread of Courtney and Lund on the stairs. They came in, closed the door behind them, and stood looking at him expectantly.

Porter said softly, 'We've got to see that neither Spain nor Vedder is caught.'

'You've got to see to it,' Courtney said. 'It's your problem, Judge, not ours.'

Porter's eyes narrowed. 'We've gone over this before. I don't know why you bring it up again. We're all in this together. You hired Vedder. Remember? The law says you're as guilty as if you had personally beaten Bowie to death.'

He paused, satisfied that some of the assurance had left the faces of the two men, then went on. 'You've got to do the jobs you're fitted for just as I have to do what I'm fitted for, and you know I can't spend days on a horse tracking Vedder and Spain. Now get some horses and go after them. Kill them, if you have to. And kill Brady Royal if it seems necessary. Just be damned sure that neither Vedder nor Spain gets back to Bear Dance.'

'So we get saddle sores while you sit here on your butt and rake the money in,' Courtney said.

'That's right, but don't forget you're raking the money in too. More than you ever made in your whole rotten lives before. Why the hell do you suppose I took you two in? For your brains? By God, no. I took you in because you can do things I can't, and this is one of them. Now get out of here and do it.'

Both stared at him angrily for a moment, then they turned and slammed out of the office.

Porter slumped in his chair. More worry. More tension. This time it could last for days. He wouldn't know whether Courtney and Lund had been successful until they returned- or until Royal did, with his prisoners.

He stared bleakly at the future. His whole life and everything he'd made of this project were at stake now, depending on Courtney and Lund doing the job he'd given them, and neither one was overly bright.

He thought of Brady Royal, of the way he had looked yesterday as he'd ridden down the street with Lee Spain as his prisoner. Royal was tough, as trail-wise as Spain and could track like an Indian.

Spain would need his hostage before he was through. Taking Shirley Ord was the one smart thing he had done, and it could be the means of beating Royal in the end. Royal certainly wouldn't do anything that would jeopardize her life.

But what about Vedder? There was

something unclean about him. There had to be something wrong with a man who could beat anyone to death the way Vedder had. And Vedder, if what Courtney had said was true, must have gone on beating the sheriff even after he was dead.

Porter wished he could go back a month or two and do everything over. Instead of sending for Spain to kill Van Schoen, he'd pay the man so much he couldn't refuse to keep quiet and go along. That, he knew now, would have been cheaper in the long run. But he couldn't go back. No man ever did.

Where would this pattern of murder end? First Van Schoen. To cover that, Van Schoen's wife and boy had died. To cover that, Sheriff Bowie had died. One thing he knew—it wasn't over yet.

Then, as happened so often lately, he asked himself why. And the answer, he told himself, was his wife. Marian was responsible for everything he had done. And she wasn't worth it. Perhaps no woman was, but least of all, Marian.

Still, he had a terrible, haunting fear that even if he got out of this trouble, he would lose her. He was sick with the thought. She was his weakness. But weakness or not, he could not go on without her.

He opened a drawer of his desk and took out a short-barreled .38. He stared at it a long time, then he replaced it and shoved the drawer back into place.

Courtney and Lund hurried toward the stable from Porter's office. Courtney said, 'Get our horses and come to the tool shed. We'll have to outfit the best we can from there. We can't risk letting anyone think we're following Royal out of town.'

Lund nodded, silent as usual. Courtney turned toward the tool shed at the edge of town, and Lund went on to the stable. Courtney wasn't looking forward to the ride ahead of him, or to spending that many days alone in Lund's company. Lund was a clod, but he was also a man to be counted on. What had happened on the street yesterday with Dude Vedder had been duplicated many times before. Courtney hadn't even had to look at Lund. He'd known Lund's gun would be in his hand, ready.

There were blankets and supplies in the tool shed. Courtney got together some blankets and threw enough provisions into a gunny sack to last several days. He hunted until he found a couple of canteens, intending to fill them when they crossed the creek before they left town, then he got two rifles and some ammunition. By the time he had finished, Lund appeared, riding one horse and leading another.

Quickly they tied the blankets and provisions behind each cantle, hung the canteens from the saddle horns, then mounted and rode out.

Courtney brooded about Porter, and about that damned Brady Royal. Because Royal hadn't killed Spain as he should have, Courtney had to make this ride, risk his neck, risk getting involved in a mess that could wind up getting him hanged . . .

Courtney had watched Royal leave town, and so had no trouble picking up Brady's trail. After a while it was joined by another, and a couple of miles farther south he came to a place where both riders had stopped and talked. Pete Ord, he guessed. Ord would be worried enough about his sister to go.

This complicated things, Courtney thought. He had intended to kill Brady Royal as the surest way of seeing that Spain and Vedder escaped. But Ord's presence with Royal would make getting the deputy just that much more difficult.

Lund said, in his deep, expressionless voice, 'Two riders.'

'Pete Ord, I figure.' Courtney shrugged, an idea coming to him. 'We'll let Brady and Ord catch 'em. If Spain and Vedder come out on top, we won't have to do nothin'. Maybe we can make sure they do come out on top. If they don't, well, we'll figure that out when the time comes. I'll tell you one thing, though. I don't much give a damn whether we plug Royal and Ord, or whether we kill Spain and Vedder to keep 'em quiet.'

CHAPTER ELEVEN

The trail of Spain, Shirley, and Vedder was not hard to follow. Apparently Spain had not even tried to hide it, counting on his hostage to hold back pursuit. Brady had suspected early this morning that Bowie's killer was Dude Vedder. Now, two hours out of Bear Dance, he found one of the conchas from Vedder's fancy pants lying in the trail, and he was sure.

The sun climbed steadily, hot and burning in the late morning sky. Heat waves rose shimmering from the land ahead, and now and then dust devils danced their uneven course across the sage.

Occasionally, under the pretense of turning to speak to Pete, Brady glanced at the trail behind. He had no illusions about having only Spain and Vedder to contend with. Porter couldn't afford any more gambling. Porter would put someone on his trail, or more than one, to see to it that Spain was not brought in again.

The chances were Porter would use Courtney and Lund. The trouble was Brady didn't know them well enough to make an intelligent guess about how they would operate. They might try to delay film, thereby giving Spain more time in which to make his escape. Perhaps, if circumstances were right, they would try to kill Spain to prevent his capture.

Shock kept Pete Ord silent until mid-morning when Brady stopped to rest and rub down the horses. Then, as Brady swung down, he said irritably, 'What the hell are you stopping for? We're not too tired to keep going.'

'That's right,' Brady said, 'but I wasn't thinking about us.'

'Well, what were you thinking about?'

'The horses. Get your saddle off and rub your horse down. Don't spare the elbow grease, either.'

Pete didn't dismount. 'To hell with babying a couple of broncs. Shirley's more important than any damned horse. Maybe she isn't to you, but she is to me.

Stifling his anger, Brady said, 'Rest that horse or you'll be afoot in another dozen miles.'

Pete glared at him sullenly, but in the end he swung off his horse, removed his saddle and with the saddle blanket began half-heartedly to rub down his horse's sweaty hide. Brady finished his own animal, then disgustedly snatched the saddle blanket from Pete and finished for him.

He returned to his saddle and Pete glared at him.

'Don't you even care what happens to Shirley? Why, right now Spain might—'

'Right now,' Brady broke in, 'he cares more about his hide than pawing Shirley.'

'But the man with him, the one who killed the sheriff . . .'

'Vedder? He'll do what Spain tells him or we'll find his carcass beside the trail. You can count on that.'

'You're so calm. Don't you have any feeling about Shirley?'

'Let me tell you something,' Brady said coldly. 'I love Shirley more than you'll ever know, more than a man like you can understand. I'm going to do my best to get her back safe. I've got a right to expect a little sense out of you about how we go at it.'

He paused. 'We might just as well face it. The chances that we can get Shirley away from them two aren't good. Spain's bad enough, but Vedder's an animal. He knows he'll hang for killing Bowie, and he can only hang once. Spain's got nothing to lose, either. But Spain's no Vedder. He's smart, he's been at this business a long time, and he's not afraid. He knows every trick in the book—maybe some that aren't in the book. If we catch him, it'll take some doin'. Now sit down and rest yourself.'

Brady waited a full half hour while Pete paced restlessly back and forth, then he got up, saddled his horse, and swung up. Pete tried to lead out, putting his horse into a lope immediately. Brady spurred forward, headed him off, and seized the headstall of his horse. 'It's too hot. We'll hold at a trot until evening when the heat lets up.'

'And lose the only chance we've—'

Brady slapped the side of his face, hard. 'What do I have to do to shut your mouth? You don't like me and you've bucked Shirley marrying me from the first. Well, I sure as hell don't like you either. Now settle down and do what I say, or by God, I'll slug you and leave you lying here without a horse. Plain enough?'

Pete nodded surlily. 'All right, all right! Now can we go?'

Brady led out without answering. He was fully aware that Pete hadn't really changed his mind, that his capitulation was only temporary. At the roadhouse tonight he'd not only have to handle Spain and Vedder, but Pete as well.

If they were lucky enough to reach the roadhouse before dark . . . before Spain and Vedder left. If they were lucky enough to find fresh horses there. If Spain and Vedder hadn't taken them all, or taken what they needed and turned the others loose . . .

The sun, reaching its zenith, was like a furnace in this rolling empty land. Ahead were the peaks of Colorado, beckoning with cool timber, with snowy caps unmelted even now in July. If Spain and Vedder reached those mountains . . . But he couldn't let himself think of that now.

Directly ahead was a sod shack, with smoke

lifting lazily from its tin chimney into the hot air. Brady altered course slightly, his eyes narrowing as he tried to make it out. It was possible that Spain and Vedder had obtained fresh horses here. It was even possible that, having made it this far, they had left Shirley, knowing they could move faster without her. It wasn't likely, though.

They rode into the ranch yard a little after one. There was a small wire corral behind the shack. It was empty, the wire gate down.

A man stepped out of the soddy and stood there, shading his eyes with a hand against the glare, staring out like a mole peering from his burrow. His hair was gray and thin, his seamed face unshaven. He stood there in his socks, a big toe sticking through one of them.

'More damn company today than I've had in a year,' he called. 'Who're you two?'

Brady reined up and sat looking down. 'Sheriff's deputy. Brady Royal's the name.' He jerked a hand toward Pete. 'This here's Pete Ord.'

'Well, you can rest a spell. Might rustle up some coffee if—'

'No thanks.' Brady shook his head. 'Two men and a woman come through here a while ago?'

'Yup. Hard lookin' feller, good lookin' woman he said was his wife, and another feller dressed like a Mex. What ye want 'em fer?'

'Murder. How long ago did they leave?'

The old man looked down at his feet. He wiggled his bare, big toe in the dust before the door. 'Oh, mebbe two, three hours. Think o' that, will ye? Killers, you say?'

'You give 'em fresh horses?'

'Now how would I do that? Ain't had a hoss in fer days.'

Brady nodded and reined his horse away. When they were out of earshot, Pete said, 'Now will you hurry? He's already passing her off as his wife.'

Brady didn't reply. If Spain was introducing Shirley as his wife, it probably meant he intended to keep her to himself. In a way, the the thought was reassuring. Brady would have been frantic if he believed Vedder was claiming her.

But what did Spain intend to do with her, once he felt he was safely away? Would he simply leave her anywhere, just to be rid of her and let her die in an empty country? Or would he make some effort to send her home?

Brady didn't know, but there was a very good possibility that Shirley's presence with Spain and Vedder might generate hostility between them. If they started fighting over her . . .

The land was rising steadily now, the plain giving way to low foothills sometimes covered with scrub cedar and jackpine. Ahead, the peaks had come out of their bluish shroud and stood starkly outlined against a sky in which clouds rode like great puffs of smoke.

The horse under Brady was tiring now and it was hard to keep him at a trot. Studying the ground, Brady could see that the three they followed were walking their horses more often than they trotted. The tracks looked fresher than they had this morning.

Brady guessed he had gained about an hour. It wasn't enough. Spain and Vedder would reach the roadhouse on the Yampa before sundown. Brady and Pete wouldn't reach it until close to dark, an hour and a half or two hours later. By that time Spain and Vedder would probably have left with Shirley.

Then, as he climbed through a particularly thick clump of cedars, he noticed something that gave him some fresh hope. One of the horses they were following was lame. It showed plainly in the tracks.

This, then, might be the edge he needed. This might give him time to catch up. He urged his horse on by touching spurs lightly to the animal's sides. Turning his head, he said, 'One of their horses is lame.'

A moment later he came to a place where either Spain or Vedder had dismounted to lift the animal's foot and examine it. From behind him Pete asked, 'You think we've got a chance?'

'We've got a better chance than we had before. We ought to gain another hour on them before sundown.'

After that he kept his horse at a steady trot, stopping only when the horse began to blow hard. They topped the pass and dropped into the drainage of the Yampa. The sun sank lower in the west, flamed briefly against the horizon, then sank out of sight.

In the gray light of dusk, Brady rounded a bend in the road and saw the log roadhouse below him on the valley floor. Immediately behind the buildings was the Yampa.

The corrals were between the buildings and the river. A half dozen or more horses were in the corral nearest the barn, perhaps more because Brady couldn't see all of it. Smoke rose lazily from the stone chimney of the house. Tied before the door were three horses. Fresh ones, Brady told himself. Horses that had come all the way from Bear Dance would have been standing hipshot, their heads down, but these were stamping and fidgeting and switching at flies with their bannered tails.

Brady swung off the road into the timber, Pete following with obvious reluctance. When they were hidden from view, Pete said, 'Let's get down there fast. We can hide ourselves at the edge of the timber. When they come out, we'll cut 'em down.'

Brady said, nothing, letting his horse pick his way carefully down the steep slope over a thick carpet of pine needles. The cooling air was heavy with the spicy fragrance of pitch and pine needles. A breeze stirred, blowing toward them from the river ahead.

Impatient with Brady's slowness to answer, Pete said, 'Well?'

'It's one way of doing it,' Brady conceded, 'but not the best way. In this light Shirley might get hit by a stray bullet. Besides, if our first shots didn't get both Spain and Vedder, they'd have us over a barrel. And dark as it is, we probably wouldn't get them the first time. They'd grab Shirley and use her for a shield. I don't aim to get caught in that kind of a squeeze.'

Pete glared at him suspiciously. 'You're bound to bring Spain in alive, ain't you?'

'I'll bring him in alive if I can,' Brady said. 'Vedder, too. The people of Bear Dance should have the privilege of trying them. They don't want a lawman to be too quick on the trigger. Remember?'

Pete swore angrily. 'After what they've done, that's a lot of hogwash.'

'Sometimes I wonder if you believe in anything,' Brady said. 'That goes for the rest of the voters in Bear Dance too.'

Pete was too angry to continue the argument. A moment later they broke out of the timber practically in the yard of the roadhouse. Brady pulled back quickly.

'We'll tie the horses here,' he said.

The yard was shrouded with dusk that would, in a few minutes, become completely dark. For a moment Brady stood motionless, studying the barn beyond the roadhouse which opened into a corral. Then, leaving the shelter of the timber, he circled behind the roadhouse at a stiff run with Pete behind him.

Spain was too old a hand at this game to leave here without getting rid of all the horses on the place. Even with Shirley as a hostage, he would know there was a possibility they'd be pursued, so he wouldn't be fool enough to leave remounts for Brady and whoever was with him.

The way Brady saw it, Spain would come here to the corral when he was through in the roadhouse. Probably he'd be alone, and Brady would have his chance to take him.

The part Brady worried about was leaving Vedder and Shirley together. But damn it, this was certainly a better plan than to go bulling in as Pete wanted to do. With any kind of luck, he could handle Spain without a gunshot, then, after a few minutes, Vedder would come out to see what was holding Spain up.

Brady stopped in the shadow of the open barn door, thinking how much in the next few minutes would depend upon luck. Pete whispered, 'What are you going to do?'

'Wait. Spain will want to get rid of all the fresh horses before he pulls out. When he comes to let 'em out of the corral, we'll take him.'

'And leave Shirley with Vedder?'

'You got a better idea?'

'You're damn right I have. I'm goin' out there into the yard. The first one who steps out of the house gets it.'

He moved from behind Brady and ran into the yard. Brady lunged after him, knowing he should have expected this. He couldn't risk having a fight on his hands with Pete when Spain left the house.

He clipped Pete solidly behind the ear with the barrel of his gun. Pete sagged, and Brady caught him under the arms. He dragged Pete back into the barn doorway and would have let him drop, but Pete steadied on his feet, and whirling, smashed Brady solidly in the mouth-with his fist.

Brady had restrained himself all day, but now his temper snapped. He ducked Pete's wild blows and sank a hard right into the man's belly just under the ribs. As Pete bent involuntarily, Brady caught him squarely in the middle of the face with an uppercut.

Pete sat down. 'You fool,' Brady said. 'Did you ride all day to fight me or to get Shirley back?'

Pete shook his head, too groggy for a moment to say anything, then muttered, 'All you want is to take Spain and Vedder back alive. You don't care a damn about Shirley.'

'All right,' Brady said wearily. 'Think what you damn please. But if you give me any more trouble, I'll cool you off for good.'

Brady turned back toward the roadhouse.

The yard was almost completely dark now. Lamplight gleamed from the dirty windows of the roadhouse, throwing a square pattern on the ground as the front door opened. Brady licked his lips and held his breath. This, he thought, would be Lee Spain.

CHAPTER TWELVE

For some time after Shirley Ord rode out of Bear Dance with Spain and Vedder, she was completely numbed by terror.

Spain led, trailing Shirley's horse. Dude Vedder brought up the rear, looking like a butcher with his blood-spattered shirt. Shirley clung to the horn of the sidesaddle. Presently the concentration and effort required just to stay on her horse dimmed her terror and she began to think again, conscious that this was no nightmare.

Their horses loped and ran and trotted under Spain's expert direction. The miles flowed steadily behind. The sun came up, driving some of the chill from Shirley's body.

She stared at Spain's back, remembering the way he had flung himself across her body early this morning when he'd invaded her bedroom. Her face burned as she recalled the way he had forced her to dress while he watched.

She remembered the brief message Spain

had scrawled on the gate with a bullet, and she realized they had no intention of killing her—yet. Dead, she would be of no value. Alive, she might be the difference between life and death to them. Spain was no fool. Hard and cold, but no fool.

Making a sudden decision, she jumped from her horse. She lit, rolling in the grass, scrambled to her feet and began to run before either Spain or Vedder had wholly recovered from their surprise.

Spain released the reins of the horse she had been riding and wheeled, but Vedder was ahead of him. He spurred toward her and flung himself from his horse. His body struck her and knocked her down.

She felt herself being yanked to her feet. Vedder's face, so close to hers, was lighted by a strange pleasure as his open hand slapped the side of her face.

Again he slapped her, holding her upright with his left hand tangled in the front of her dress.

She heard Spain's harsh voice: 'Vedder! Let her go.'

But he didn't obey. The blows kept up, and she knew, suddenly, that this man before her was no man at all, but a twisted animal bearing the appearance of a man. She also knew that this slapping was, for Vedder, a prelude to murder.

The slapping stopped abruptly, and Shirley

fell away. Spain yanked her to her feet. Vedder lay in the grass, half conscious, his scalp bleeding where Spain had struck him with his gun barrel.

'Damn you,' Spain said, 'what are you trying to do? Make up your mind to it, you can't get away and I won't let you hold us up any more. Try another crazy trick like that and I'll let Vedder do what he wants with you.'

Shirley, realizing he meant exactly what he said, only nodded. Then Spain whirled on Vedder. He kicked the man savagely in the ribs. 'Get up. Another stupid trick like that and I'll tie you up and leave you. You make me sick, anyway. I don't much like what you done to the sheriff, either. This girl's the only chance we've got. You keep your slimy hands off her.'

Shirley recognized his inconsistency, but didn't find it very funny. He had threatened her with Vedder, then had turned around and threatened Vedder if he touched her again.

Spain went to her horse and led him back. He helped her into the saddle. Leading the horse, he went to his own and mounted. Vedder got up, shaking his head as though to clear it. He got on his horse without speaking, and Spain led out again.

Shirley glanced around once at Vedder's face. The expression told her that the only chance she had of getting through this alive depended upon Spain continuing to dominate

Vedder.

They rode again, in grim silence. Spain, Shirley realized, was rattled. He was angry over the killing of the sheriff, a useless act which he knew would intensify Brady Royal's efforts to catch him. Perhaps he was also worried about kidnapping her. He must know that any harm done to her would insure Brady forever hunting him down.

She thought about Brady and realized he would come after her regardless of Spain's warning. He might, though, be more cautious in the way he went about his pursuit. He would probably come alone, wouldn't trust her safety to the unthinking anger of a posse. Yes, he'd come alone. But he'd come. She was sure of that.

So it was up to her to delay Spain and Vedder as much as she could, in any way she could. The single effort she'd made to delay them had been dealt with harshly, but she'd made them lose some twenty minutes. Twenty minutes here and twenty there might add up to enough to mean the difference between success and failure for Brady . . .

They reached a sod shack about ten and rode in. Spain cautioned her as they approached it: 'You're my wife as far as any strangers are concerned. And if you're thinking about trying to get anybody to help you, remember how easy it will be for me to kill them.'

111

'Killing is all that you think about, isn't it?'

She saw that the remark angered him. 'I don't enjoy it, if that's what you mean. I'm not Vedder.'

An old man came to the door of the shack. Spain said, 'Howdy. We're heading south into Colorado. Whereabouts would be the first place we could get fresh horses?'

'Johnson's roadhouse. On the Yampa. 'Bout forty miles straight south.'

'Got any coffee?'

'Might.'

'Fetch it out.'

The old man glanced from Spain to Vedder and back again, then went into the soddy. Spain nodded at Vedder. 'Go in with him.'

Vedder stepped down and went into the shack. Presently the old man returned with a pot of coffee and three tin cups, Vedder following. Spain motioned at Shirley. 'All right. Get down. Stretch a little and drink some coffee.'

Shirley slid to the ground. She accepted a cup from the old man. She looked away, fighting an urge to tell him about her trouble, but she couldn't risk warning him even with her eyes. She knew it would bother neither Spain nor Vedder to leave the old man dead. And they would kill him, she thought, if they had the slightest hint that something was wrong.

The coffee was too strong and only

lukewarm, but she drank it gratefully. When she finished, Spain said, 'All right. Get back into the saddle. Time we was moving.'

Vedder stared at her from the ground, licked dry lips. Spain took the reins of her horse and led out. Vedder mounted and fell in behind her. The old man watched from the door of his soddy, frowning against the sun.

There wasn't much anyone could do, Shirley told herself. She would go on and on with the two men until, inevitably, they began to fight with each other. And then what? She had felt the lust in Spain this morning; she had felt it in Vedder all day.

There was little choice between them, but she found herself hoping it would be Vedder who was killed. If Spain survived, she would at least have some chance.

And she realized something else. Men like these two could not exist if it weren't for the men who hired them, who protected them and helped them break jail when they were caught. It was a strange thing that she had been unable to understand this in the safety of her home. She should have told Brady she understood instead of arguing with him and asking him to give up his star . . .

In mid-afternoon Spain called for a stop to rest the horses and water them in a near-dry creek that meandered across the sage-covered flat. There were locusts growing along the bank, and one of their thorns pricked her hand as she reached out to steady herself.

Something out of a long-dead past came back to her. She remembered a pony she had ridden as a girl that had gone lame. Her father had extracted a thorn from the frog of the pony's hoof. Carefully, so they wouldn't notice what she was doing, she twisted the thorn loose from the tree. It was about an inch long.

Spain was lying down, his hat over his face. The horses stamped and switched their tails in the sandy bed of the creek. Vedder watched Shirley with eyes as forbidding as a snake's. Shirley got up and headed self-consciously for the creek behind the screen of brush. Vedder rose lazily to follow.

Shirley said, her face reddening, 'Mr. Spain, I'd like to go down to the creek and be alone for a few minutes. Will you make *him* stay here?'

Spain lifted his hat off his face, grinning. Vedder snickered. 'I was just goin' to watch her,' he said.

'Let her alone. She ain't goin' nowhere.'

Vedder stopped. He plucked a twig from a tree and put one end of it into his mouth. Shirley felt his eyes on her until she was out of sight behind a screen of brush.

She went immediately to the horse she had been riding and lifted one of his front hoofs gingerly. She wasn't used to this, but she'd seen it done often enough. You just tugged on the fetlock hair, and if the horse was trained at all, he lifted his foot for you.

It worked. She shoved the thorn into a crack in the frog. It didn't go all the way in, but it was the best she could do. Maybe it would work in deeper as he walked.

She stayed until she heard Spain call, 'Hurry up, damn it. We can't wait all day.' Then she returned to them.

Vedder got the horses and Spain again helped her mount. They rode south keeping the same steady pace they had all day.

Shirley waited for her horse to go lame, but he didn't. She supposed that the thorn had worked out instead of in. If she'd only been a little stronger, or if she'd known exactly where to place it. It was hopeless. Brady wasn't coming, and even if he was, he'd never catch them. The way Spain was pushing the horses, they'd be nearly dead by the time it was dark. Obviously Spain intended to get fresh horses at Johnson's roadhouse and keep riding all night.

Even Shirley, who had been raised in town, knew it was impossible to trail anything in the dark. That meant Brady would have to wait for dawn. By that time Spain and Vedder would have a ten- or twelve-hour lead, one that Brady could never make up.

But in late afternoon, her horse began to limp. Spain swung down and lifted the horse's hoof. He extracted the thorn, cursing softly. He remounted and went on, but at a slower pace, for Shirley's horse continued to limp and pulled back constantly against the reins in Spain's hand.

Again the hours dragged by. The sun sank toward the western rim of the land until, with just a red arc showing above the distant hills, they rode down a long, timbered slope and saw the Yampa ahead.

They rode into the yard of Johnson's place along the road, Spain stopping at the front door. A man came out and Spain said, 'I want three fresh horses. I'll pick 'em out. Then we'll eat and go on.'

The man nodded and accompanied Spain to the corral behind the main building. Vedder chewed on a needle he had picked from a pine and coolly studied Shirley.

'I had to slap you around some this morning,' Vedder said. 'Spain expected it. The only reason I did it was to cover up the way I feel about you.'

She didn't reply.

After a moment Vedder went on. 'You know what he'll do with you when he don't figure he needs you any more?'

Still Shirley didn't answer.

Vedder's voice became angry. 'He'll kill you. That's what he'll do. Now if you was to be a little nice to me, I'd try, an' help you get away from him.'

'Would you like me to tell Mr. Spain what you just said?'

'By God, you'd better not.'

'Then don't say anything about it again.'

'All right! But I'm the only chance you've got. I thought—'

Spain, leading three fresh horses, returned with the man from the roadhouse. 'Go on inside,' he said. 'We'll eat fast and get out of here.'

Shirley knew she should warn Spain. Vedder might shoot him in the back any time. The thought of being at Vedder's mercy turned the chill in her spine into a live thing. But she didn't say anything. She wouldn't mention it yet. Maybe after they had eaten. Maybe telling Spain would start a fight between them, a fight that would delay their departure.

Whatever she did to help herself had to be done within the next few hours . . .

CHAPTER THIRTEEN

As Brady watched, Spain moved through the door of Johnson's roadhouse. He instantly stepped aside into the shadows beside the door, becoming invisible there.

Brady's hatred of the man rose in his throat. Trust Spain's instinct to move him out of the light from the door. The outlaw was more wolf than man.

'Where'd he go?' Pete whispered. 'Where's

Vedder and Shirley?'

Brady didn't reply. His eyes tried to pierce the darkness, his mind tried to guess what Spain would do. Would he come here to the corral as Brady expected him to? Or would he take a chance on leaving without releasing the fresh horses in the corral?

Brady said softly, 'Come on,' and moved out from the shadows into the yard.

This, he knew, was a touchy business at best. Somewhere in the roadhouse were Vedder and Shirley. Spain was hiding over there by the door. Brady could not guess what was in the man's mind, but he knew he couldn't just stand by and let the three of them ride away. Anything could happen during the long night ahead.

Movement in the timber across the clearing caught his eyes. Was it possible that Spain had crossed the yard to the fringe of trees without being seen? Brady doubted it. Again he remembered his earlier thought that Porter would send someone, probably Courtney and Lund, to see that Spain was not captured alive again.

Brady caught someone's blurred movement by the front door of the roadhouse. The door was still open, light streaming through it on the ground in front of the house. Brady cursed the lack of light in the yard. Shooting was impossible in this kind of light. It was guesswork. A hit would be sheer luck. Nothing

118

more.

Where was Vedder? And Shirley? And where was Lee Spain now? Had he moved? Or was he still there by the door?

A vague figure moved away from the shadow of the main building and merged with the dim shapes of the horses tied to the rail. Spain! He was untying the horses. In a minute or two Vedder would come through the door with Shirley.

Now Brady knew that his only chance was to kill Vedder as the man stepped through the doorway. He didn't have a chance of taking Vedder alive. This was no time to consider an intangible such as due process of law. For Shirley's sake, he had to kill Dude Vedder, and he'd get no more than one shot to do the job.

He might not even get that one shot. If Vedder was as shrewd as Spain, he'd come through the door with Shirley in front of him. Once they stepped out of the light, Brady's chance would be gone.

Brady stopped in the middle of the yard, fully aware that he was visible there, at least as an indistinct shape. Pete bumped him from behind and grunted with surprise.

Now Brady heard Spain's voice, low and urgent, calling to Vedder inside the house. 'Someone's out here. Keep that damn girl close to you as you come out. Get clear of the light quick as you can. The horses are ready.'

Vedder appeared in the doorway, moving

fast, Shirley held against him, his arm around her. Brady raised his gun from reflex, but his finger didn't tighten on the trigger. The danger of hitting Shirley was so great—he couldn't risk a shot.

A gun flared from the edge of the timber beyond the roadhouse. An instant later the sound of the report reached Brady's ears, the deep bellow of a rifle. The bullet struck the doorjamb and showered Shirley and Vedder with splinters. Then both were out of the lighted doorway and running toward the horses, hidden by the darkness.

The rifle fared again, and, like an echo, a pistol barked. Two of them, Courtney and Lund, sure as hell.

Brady opened up on the muzzle flashes, forced into it by his concern for Shirley. He triggered three fast shots, then ran toward the door of the roadhouse.

He could hear the nervous movements of the horses, the creak of stirrup leather as someone swung to the saddle. He heard Spain's low cursing. Damn them. Maybe he'd still get a shot at one of them if he could reach them in time. They couldn't ride with Shirley clutched against them as a shield. They had three horses. Shirley had been riding one.

He'd try to shoot Shirley's horse out from under her. She might be hurt in the fall, but measured against the hurt that waited for her in the night ahead, a fall would be nothing.

The rifle and revolver in the timber opened up again. A bullet seared Brady's thigh, and behind him, Pete let out a long, high yell of pain. Brady heard him fall and groan as he rolled over flat on his belly.

Brady didn't stop or slow down. Ahead of him Shirley screamed, and the horses thundered away from the dark shape of the building. In that exact moment Courtney and Lund opened up again, firing wildly.

Brady stopped, sliding, and steadied himself. He raised his gun, then held his fire. He couldn't see the sights; he could only aim by feel. And suddenly he realized he couldn't tell them apart: Shirley, Spain, Vedder—all three were crouched, lumped shapes upon the backs of running horses. He didn't dare shoot at a rider because the one he fired at might be Shirley.

Now they were a hundred feet away from him. They had crossed the yard before him, and became blurred and indistinct shapes, rapidly fading into the darkness. He fired three fast shots, low, hoping to hit one of the horses in the leg. Then they were gone, fading into the timber on the far side of the clearing.

Pete, lying on the ground in the middle of the clearing, groaned helplessly. Brady whirled and sprinted toward the fringe of timber where he had left the horses. Callous as it seemed, he had to leave Pete, trusting that the people in the roadhouse would take care of him. If he

121

could get on Spain's trail soon enough, he might pressure him into making a mistake. At least he could learn the direction Spain and Vedder were taking if he could pick up the sound of their passage.

But he didn't reach the horses. A man stepped from the door of the roadhouse, a lantern held high in his hand, its lights reaching beyond Brady, beyond Pete, and on into the darkness. Instantly Courtney or Lund opened up again.

Brady started running, weaving, trying to upset the aim of the two men at the edge of the timber. He'd never reach darkness before they tagged him, he thought. He was acutely aware of Pete, lying unprotected in the open.

He turned and shouted at the man in front of the roadhouse, 'Put that damned lantern out.' He dived behind a smashed packing crate that lay in the center of the yard. It was doubtful shelter; a bullet from the big rifle would tear through the flimsy wood, but at least they couldn't see him.

He hugged the ground, and poking his gun around the side of the crate, waited. When the rifle flared again, he shot at the burst of powder flame that ribboned out briefly into the darkness. His hammer clicked on an empty.

Cursing, Brady rolled onto his side and thumbed cartridges from his belt into the cylinder. He put in five, rolled back onto his belly, and poked the gun around the corner.

The man from the roadhouse was still standing there with the lantern, probably so befuddled by fear that he didn't know what to do. Brady yelled at him again, 'Blow that damn thing out.'

Courtney's voice, raised angrily, came clearly across the yard from the timber, 'Don't move, mister.'

The man froze, lantern held aloft. Courtney fired again, the bullet tearing through the packing crate inches from Brady's head. The man with him, Lund no doubt, began firing with his revolver at Pete, who was stirring feebly on the ground.

They had Brady hipped, behind a packing crate which was no protection at all, yet if he struck out for the dark shadows around the barn and corrals, or for the brush along the river, they'd cut him down before he went ten feet. On the other hand, if he stayed where he was, a bullet would find him and Pete unless the damned lantern was put out.

He'd already lost the slight margin of time that might have kept him on Spain's trail. No chance now to follow by sound. All he could do was wait and stay alive, if he could. He raised his revolver and took a careful bead on the lantern. It wobbled and swayed. The man's arm must have been tiring, but he was afraid to lower it.

Brady steadied his gun hand with the other

123

hand. Carefully he eased back the hammer, held his breath, and fired. The slug smashed the lantern, knocking it out of the man's hand and sending it flying through the air a dozen feet.

Brady was on his feet immediately and running toward the timber where Courtney and Lund had been hiding. As he raced toward them, he triggered a couple of fast shots in their direction. But they had no stomach for a close quarters' fight. Or perhaps they had thought they had given Spain the time he needed to make his escape. Brady heard them scrambling up the slope through the trees. As he reached the edge of the timber, he heard their horses pounding up the slope.

He stopped and, swinging around wearily, returned to where Pete lay. He knelt beside Pete. 'Where are you hurt?' he asked.

'Leg. I think it's broke. Oh God, give me something for the pain. It's killin' me.'

Brady called, 'You over there. The one with the lantern. Come here.'

He heard the man's steps approach cautiously through the darkness. When he stopped a few feet away, Brady said, 'Help me get this man inside.'

Between them, they lifted Pete, who fainted immediately. Dragging his feet, they crossed the yard to the front door and went inside.

This room, the main one, was forty feet long and half as wide. An enormous rock fireplace, blackened by smoke, was at one end. There was a long plank table for eating in the center of the room, and several leather-covered couches in front of the fireplace. They laid Pete down on one of the couches as a white woman and an Indian girl watched from the kitchen doorway.

'The shooting's over,' Brady said. 'Nothing to be afraid of now. Get some whisky—quick.'

The woman brought him a half-filled brown bottle. Brady looked at Pete, who was still unconscious, then took a stiff slug from the bottle himself. He set the bottle on the floor beside the couch, and taking out his pocket knife, slit Pete's pants leg from cuff to thigh.

Pete had been wrong about the bone being broken. The bullet had passed through the fleshy part of the thigh, perhaps glancing off the bone but not shattering it. The wound was bleeding, but it was a steady bleeding rather than spurts, which would have indicated an artery had been cut. If that had happened, Pete would likely have bled to death by now. Barring gangrene, Pete was in no danger, but he wouldn't be riding a horse for weeks to come. Now he'd have to stay behind.

Brady turned to the woman. She was untidy and slatternly, her shoulders bent by hard work, the skin of her hands rough and cracked, her gaunt face mute evidence of daily privations.

'Fetch me some clean towels,' he said.

She turned without a word, as if she was used to obeying orders, and trudged wearily toward the kitchen. While he waited, Brady took another slug from the bottle. It steadied him, but it could not dull his gnawing fear for Shirley or his consuming hatred for Spain and Vedder. And there was the bitter sense of guilt.

He'd had his chance, and he'd failed. It was no good to say that his plan would probably have worked if it hadn't been for Courtney and Lund, or if the roadhouse man hadn't come out with his lantern. The hard fact remained that—he had been here within a few feet of Shirley, and they'd escaped with her. She was in the same danger she'd been in all day, perhaps worse now that Spain had come so close to being caught.

The woman returned with the towels. Brady took them, glad of the chance to do something and for the moment get his mind off Shirley. He put a towel under Pete's wounded leg, then poured most of the remaining whisky on the wound. He wrapped it carefully with another towel, then tore a third one into strips with which he bandaged it.

Pete opened his eyes as Brady finished. Brady slid an arm under his head and raised it. Tipping the bottle, Brady poured Pete's mouth full of whisky. Pete coughed, some of the whisky dribbling down his chin, but he succeeded in swallowing most of it. Then he fainted again.

Brady turned away, and fishing for the makings, rolled a cigarette. He crossed the room to the fireplace, and sat down to wait with his bitter thoughts.

CHAPTER FOURTEEN

Brady waited an hour. He smoked three cigarettes, but he found no comfort in them. Occasionally Pete stirred or groaned, but he remained only half conscious. Brady knew there was a great deal of shock connected with a bullet wound, and that it would take a while before Pete got over it. He hoped he'd get a chance to talk to Pete before he left at dawn, and then his thoughts returned to Shirley.

He rose and began pacing back and forth across the room. He could hear the sounds from the kitchen as the women prepared his supper. The man who ran the roadhouse, Johnson, the same fellow who had held the lantern outside, had disappeared.

Brady wondered what Courtney and Lund would do. Probably they had camped for the night somewhere in the timber. When dawn came, they would pick up the trail too.

Brady could guess what Porter's orders to them had been: *Don't let Brady Royal take either Spain or Yedder alive.* They'd be after

Spain and Vedder as anxiously as Brady was, but there would be an important difference. They wouldn't care anything about Shirley's safety.

He doubted if they were much danger to himself, for the present at least. True, they had fired at him and Pete, but it seemed logical to think they had done it to prevent his taking Spain and Vedder. Probably they would have preferred Spain and Vedder as targets.

Still, Brady wasn't sure of that. He had frankly disliked Courtney because of his connection with Porter, and he had plainly showed that dislike. Courtney had clearly resented Brady's treatment. It was possible, then, that Courtney would find a good deal of satisfaction in drawing a bead on Brady's back.

Brady's mouth twisted. Spain had taken Porter's money for killing the Van Schoens. Later on Vedder had been paid to break Spain out of jail. Now Porter's money was trying to buy their deaths. And only Brady was interested in keeping them alive—until they'd implicated Porter and a noose was around all their necks . . .

By the time Brady finished eating, Pete was fully conscious. Brady got up from the table and walked to the couch where Pete lay. The fight had gone out of the storekeeper. His face was gray with the weakness and pain of his wound. His eyes were narrowed, his mouth compressed.

128

'Get her away from them, Brady. For God's sake, get her away from them.'

Brady nodded.

'You're different than me,' Pete said. 'If anybody can get Shirley from them, you can. I know that. I guess I knew it all along.'

That was quite an admission coming from Pete Ord, and it brought a spare smile to Brady's face. He said, 'Thanks. I'll do my best. Don't forget I love her too. You'll have to stay here till your wound gets better. I'll get word back to you whenever I can.'

Brady went outside and took care of the horses. Returning to the big room, he stretched out on one of the couches, closed his eyes and instantly went to sleep.

*   *   *

When Brady woke, it was still pitch-black. He was stiff from the uncomfortable couch, but he was rested. The room was dark. Moving quietly, Brady crossed to the front door and went outside.

The air was sharp with the night chill. There was a hint of gray in the east just above the horizon, and impatience stirred in hint. He had to be on the move.

Walking to the barn, he found a lantern and lighted it. He looked at the horses he and Pete had ridden, and decided he'd rather take them than risk getting stung in a horse trade. They

129

had rested all night. Riding one and trading the other, he could change off from time to time, thus keeping both animals in reasonably good shape.

He saddled his own horse, leaving Pete's saddle behind. He put about twenty-five pounds of oats into a gunny sack and tied it behind his saddle, then led the horses into the dark yard.

The gray was stronger in the east now. A lamp went on in the house, moved through it and ended up in the kitchen. Brady went to the back door and knocked.

Johnson opened it, clad only in his pants and underwear and boots. Brady said, 'I took twenty-five pounds of oats. Send your bill for everything to Bear Dance County. And take good care of Pete.'

The man nodded. 'There's a doctor over at the Hahn's Peak diggings. Want me to send for him?'

Brady nodded. 'Do that. Pete's got a nasty wound.'

The man shifted uneasily from one foot to the other. 'I'm sorry about that lantern last night. If I'd knowed what was goin' on—'

'Forget it. I'm sorry I had to shoot the lantern out of your hand. Get hurt?'

'Couple of cuts is all. Come on in, Deputy. I'll have coffee in a minute.'

Brady shook his head. 'No, I'll be going.'

'Good luck.'

Brady nodded and turned away. Mounting, he rode out in the direction Spain and Vedder had gone last night. He couldn't see the ground, so he reined in where the timber began.

He waited until the sky grew lighter then, when he could see the trail, he rode on. It crossed the river and climbed out of the Yampa Valley, heading straight south. The hoof marks were deep, indicating that the horses had been lunging up the slope, cruelly spurred.

Brady kept a steady pace, saving his horses as much as he could. Spain and Vedder already had a six-hour lead. He wouldn't make that up in a day and there was no sense killing his horses trying. More than that, the country to the south was rough and held practically no settlers this side of White River, so it was doubtful if he would find a place where he could obtain fresh horses.

The land lifted steadily from the river, raising in a series of ridges and ravines instead of tipping up in one long, continuous grade. In places he hit patches of pine where the trail became all but invisible because of the heavy carpeting of needles that covered the ground.

Occasionally Brady could see the marching line of snow-capped sentinel peaks to the east that marked the Continental Divide. And westward, he caught occasional glimpses of the vast expanse of Utah desert.

Brady tried to put himself in Spain's place, to think the way Spain would think. Two facts were obvious: Spain would keep Shirley as a hostage to use as a bargaining agent if his luck turned sour and Brady caught up with him; and he would continue in a more or less southerly direction. He was unlikely to swing east and try to cross the Continental Divide over one of the high passes, and it seemed equally unlikely that he would turn west where the Utah desert was rugged even for those who know the country well.

Probably Spain would keep going south across White River and on to the Grand, perhaps swinging down-river to its junction with the Gunnison, then up the Gunnison to the big mining camps of the San Juan, where he could lose himself in the crowd of milling strangers that came and went by the hundreds. Once there, his trail would be hard to follow. He wouldn't need Shirley, so . . . But Brady's thinking stopped short of that finality. He'd catch up with Spain before he reached the San Juan. He had to.

The sun rose, the heat beating down upon the brooding pines and filling the air with pungent fragrance. Brady's horse snorted and reared at a black bear ahead in the trail. A herd of elk, fifty or more, spooked from Brady's approach and crashed thunderously through the timber away from him. Partridges drummed from pine to pine, startling Brady with the sudden beat of their wings.

Shirley must have given up hope by now, Brady thought. Very likely she thought that Brady had been killed or wounded by Courtney or Lund. He pictured her in his mind, and he pictured Spain and Vedder, and felt his anger, always close to the surface now, boil up in him again.

Sooner or later Spain and Vedder would quarrel over Shirley. When they did, one or the other might be killed. Brady caught himself praying that Spain would stay alert, that he wouldn't be caught napping when the showdown came. Brady had never imagined he would ever pray for Lee Spain, yet he was doing it now.

The sun climbed steadily into the eastern sky, its dry heat beating upon the land. Then, in a small valley formed by a creek, he came upon the tracks of two horses that had crossed the stream and turned into the trail Brady himself was following. The tracks were about two hours old.

Courtney and Lund! Instead of camping near the roadhouse as he had thought they would, they'd ridden blindly south all through the night as Brady had at first considered doing, gambling on being able to pick up the trail in the morning. They'd won, too, but they'd made a bad trade. They'd given a night's rest for themselves and their horses for a two-hour advantage this morning.

While he regretted even this small advantage they'd gained, Brady knew that if he had it to do over again, he would do exactly as he had last night. He had made his reputation by painstaking patience and care, not by guessing and gambling and going off half-cocked.

Still, their two-hour advantage complicated Brady's task. If Spain and Vedder were caught today, Courtney and Lund would catch them first. The thought turned Brady cold, though a more logical part of him realized how unlikely it was that such would be the case. But if they did manage to catch Spain and Vedder, Shirley wouldn't have a chance. They couldn't afford to let her live. Not only would she be a witness to their killing of the pair, but she would certainly have heard enough talk from Spain and Vedder to know and testify that they were tied in with Porter.

Brady caught himself hurrying his horses beyond the pace they were able to maintain. Deliberately he slowed down. There was only one way to do this, he told himself. A few extra minutes gained at the expense of exhaustion for his horses would be a costly and senseless gain.

He rode all afternoon, keeping a wary eye on the clouds that were building up steadily over the distant desert to the west. Slowly the ponderous cloud mass moved eastward toward the towering peaks. They might dump rain as they passed overhead, or they might go on, leaving the country dry.

Brady was not one to indulge in wishful thinking, but he realized that was what he was doing now. He knew what the clouds could do. The smell and the feel of rain was in the air now. The deluge would come, destroying forever the trail he followed.

The sun was blotted out a few minutes later. The clouds, dark and sullenly gray, spread across the sky. Then it began to rain, lightly at first, then with increasing tempo. Lightning flashed and thunder rolled across the land. Brady's horses laid back their ears in mute protest.

Then the rain came in great sheets, screening even the next ridge ahead of Brady. The ground grew slick, and both horses floundered trying to maintain their footing. Within a few minutes, the ever dimming trail of Spain and Vedder and Shirley Ord was gone.

Brady was out of Wyoming and in a country where he had no legal status, but that made no difference. It made no difference, either, that he might be needed back in Bear Dance where, now that Frank Bowie was dead, there was no law.

He only knew he would not give up the pursuit. If rescue was impossible, then, by God, he'd have revenge.

CHAPTER FIFTEEN

Riding away from Johnson's roadhouse, Spain kept a tight hold on Shirley's reins, dragging her horse along while Vedder crowded it from behind. He saw the blur that was Brady Royal out in the middle of the yard, saw the flashes of Royal's gun. Then they were into the timber beyond the clearing, and pounding through it.

He cursed continuously as they rode. The girl was not as valuable a hostage as he had supposed. Apparently his threat against her life hadn't bothered Royal. At least it hadn't kept the deputy off the trail.

The two men who had fired at Royal from the timber puzzled him for a moment, and then he understood. Porter must have sent Courtney and Lund to make sure that neither he nor Vedder was captured. His and Vedder's lives meant nothing to Porter. The judge would be interested in only one thing—to be sure that there would be no evidence against him and dead men didn't testify.

Still, the only thing Spain was really sure about was that Brady Royal was on his trail. The man with Royal had been hit. That reduced the odds, but it didn't help much. The trouble was, Spain knew Brady Royal. The man would keep to his trail like a leech.

The branch of a pine slapped his chest,

raked his face, and nearly brushed him from the saddle. Behind him, Shirley cried out in pain as the same branch tore at her.

They crossed the river and turned south. After that Spain gave his attention to the land ahead, dodging the clawing branches of the pines, avoiding deadfalls and other obstacles that tended to slow them down.

The night hours passed. At dawn Spain called a halt long enough for coffee and a quick breakfast, then went on again. He judged he had a six-hour lead, which should put twenty miles between them and Brady Royal. Later today he'd take time to hide their trail. But not yet. At this altitude there was a good chance they'd get rain.

Glancing back, Spain saw that Shirley clung wearily to her saddle. She wasn't used to long hours in the saddle, but to hell with that. He wouldn't let her slow them up again. Not if he had to tie her across the saddle like the carcass of a deer.

The country was strange to Spain, and grew more rugged as the hours passed. Spain knew none of them could keep this pace up. Sooner or later they would have to stop and rest.

Spain watched the build-up of clouds over the Utah desert with keen interest, watched their slow drift eastward toward the peaks. When it started to rain, his tension eased and he felt wonderfully relieved. The rain had saved him. It would blot out twenty miles of trail between him and Brady Royal.

Now he angled westward, deliberately picking thick patches of timber through which to ride, knowing that the heavy carpet of pine needles on the ground would effectively hide their tracks.

The clouds passed on overhead, and presently the sun came out, low in the western sky. They kept on through the chill, damp air. He didn't want to sleep on the wet ground tonight. He wanted a roof over his head. Not that there was much chance of finding one, but it wouldn't hurt to keep riding until dusk in the hope of finding a dry place to sleep.

He had nearly given up hope of finding such a refuge when, at dusk, he saw in the distance the remnant of an old pole fence and a sod-roofed log cabin. He reined up immediately, calling back, 'Get down and rest. I'll scout the cabin. If it's empty, we can spend the night there.'

The other two stopped. Shirley slid off her horse. Her legs collapsed under her and she fell with a moan. Vedder dismounted, for once having no interest in the girl. He stumbled and fell, lay there, his eyes closed.

Spain stared sourly at the pair. He was tired and sleepy and hungry, but he was a long way from the shape Vedder was in. For all of his fancy duds, this one wasn't much man. Spain expected this complete exhaustion in Shirley, but not Vedder. Damn it, they were millstones

138

around his neck. He'd be better off to leave them—now—tonight. He could get away, now that he had this lead.

He turned this thought over in his mind as he rode cautiously toward the weathered cabin. He saw no signs of life, no fresh tracks as he rode in.

The door was ajar, the cabin dark. Spain dismounted before the cabin and stepped inside, gun in hand. A musty smell greeted him. Rats scurried away. Mice rustled overhead in the brush and poles that supported the sod roof.

Spain stepped beck outside. An abandoned cow camp. From the appearance of the place, he judged that no one had been here for months.

He mounted and sat his saddle, staring at the cabin, then back at the others. He knew what would happen to Shirley if he left her with Vedder for any length of time. She'd be dead by morning—if she were lucky. Royal would find her, and in time would find Vedder.

And Spain knew that if he abandoned Shirley to Vedder, Royal wouldn't quit until he found him. He'd follow Spain if it took the rest of his life.

He turned his horse and rode slowly back to where he had left Shirley and Vedder. They'd sleep here tonight. Maybe hole up and rest for several days to let the horses recover their strength. Then they'd go on. He'd try to leave

Shirley some place where she'd be safe. If Royal got her back safely, he might give up following a cold trail.

But would Royal forget what happened to his brother? Or the Van Schoens? Or Frank Bowie? It didn't make any difference that Vedder, not Spain, had murdered Bowie. Indirectly Lee Spain had been responsible for the sheriff's death. At least that was the way Royal would see it. But those were minor crimes measured against what would happen to Shirley if Spain left her in Vedder's hands. No, he couldn't leave Shirley and Vedder, because that was the one thing that would make Royal forget he was a deputy.

Spain cursed softly. If Royal ever got close enough, Spain would do what he should have done yesterday. He'd lay an ambush and shoot Royal as he rode past. In that way only could he be sure he'd get the man off his back. If that happened, he wouldn't give a damn about what Vedder did to the girl.

*　　　*　　　*

Shirley Ord was completely exhausted when she reached the cabin. She didn't want to eat—didn't want to do anything but collapse and sleep. Even her terror had dulled with exhaustion.

Vedder was equally exhausted, Spain not much better. They didn't even bother to build

140

a fire in the rusty sheet-iron stove. Spain picketed the horses out to graze, then he and Vedder rolled up in their blankets and lay down to sleep.

Shirley wrapped herself in the blanket that Spain had grudgingly given her, and lay down against a far wall, as far from the men as she could get. It was moldy smelling in here, and she heard the mice overhead. They weren't important. What was important was the fact that Spain was between her and Vedder.

A coyote barked somewhere in the night, a lonely, eerie sound. But her fatigue was so great that she fell asleep almost instantly, and did not awaken until Spain shook her shoulder the following morning.

A fire was blazing in the stove. She got up, stiff and sore, and limped outside. She couldn't stand another day of riding, she told herself. No matter what Spain did to her, she wouldn't get on a horse today.

The early morning air was clear and winy, fragrant with spruce and pungent sage. Shirley stumbled to the spring and washed her face. She had no comb, so she ran her fingers through her tangled hair. A screen of brush separated her from the cabin, and she was thankful that the men stayed inside until she returned.

She hated them so much that for the moment she forgot she was afraid of them, and said to Spain, 'If you're far enough from Brady

141

to risk a fire, you're far enough away to let me go.'

Spain grinned, and said with mock regret, 'Shucks, I thought you were beginning to like us. Well, I could let you go, I guess.' Spain glanced slyly at Vedder. 'I could leave you with Dude.'

Vedder's face was drawn with weariness, but now his eyes brightened and Shirley sensed clearly what was in his mind.

Spain laughed. 'Dude would like it, even if you didn't.'

He poured coffee into three tin cups and they drank it black, along with some dried biscuits and cold meat he had obtained at Johnson's roadhouse. The Johnson woman must not have expected them to come back; she had pawned off some moldy biscuits and meat that was turning bad. Shirley choked it down. She was weak with hunger, and she knew she would need all the strength she could get.

But Spain ate only part of his. He got up disgustedly from the table, rinsed his mouth out with coffee and spat it on the dirt floor. 'To hell with this,' he said. 'It's bad enough to run, but I'll be damned if I'm going to starve too. Not with two thousand dollars in my pocket.'

Vedder looked up. 'That's more'n ten times what I got for breakin' you out.'

'You wasn't paid for killing,' Spain said.

'You done yours for fun.'

Vedder started to get up, but Spain pushed him back and stared at Vedder until the younger man's gaze shifted. Then he said, 'I'm going to look for a settlement. I might be gone all day, but then again I might be back in an hour or two if I'm lucky. While I'm gone, keep your dirty paws off this girl or I'll blow your damn head off when I get back. Savvy?'

Vedder's reply was a surly grunt. Spain reached down and took Vedder by the shoulders and shook him until his teeth rattled. 'I changed my mind. I won't blow your head off. I'll take my knife and cut your heart out. If you try to make a run for it, I'll track you and I'll catch you. She belongs to me. I've beefed more'n one man who tried to get to my women. You got it through your head now?'

'Yeah,' Vedder mumbled.

Spain picked up his rifle and went outside. Shirley ran after him and caught him twenty feet from the door. 'You're not going to leave me with him?'

'He won't touch you. I warned him. He knows what will happen if—'

'You think that will stop him? He's not a man. You know that.'

'Maybe you think you're prettier than you are.'

'But—'

'Ah, shut up,' he said, and walked away.

She returned to the cabin and sat down

against the outside wall. The sun beat against her. The earth, soaked from the rain the day before, steamed under the morning sun. No sound except the natural sounds of the forest: a jay calling from somewhere back in the timber, a woodpecker beating a tattoo against a tree trunk. Looking around at this wild, peaceful land, it was hard to believe her danger was so real.

Spain rode away to the southwest. Vedder came out, chewing on a match. He rolled the match back and forth and watched Spain until he was lost in the timber. Then he looked at Shirley.

'I could wait yonder by that big pine for him to come back,' Vedder said. 'Be easy to shoot him as he rides up. He's fixing to kill you, girlie, just as soon as he figures he don't need you no more. Unless I kill him first.'

Shirley, met his, gaze. 'I'll warn him if you try it, and he'll kill you instead.'

'The man ain't been born that can kill me,' he boasted. 'And I've had better women than you, too. Women that wanted me.'

He had changed in the few seconds since Spain had ridden out of sight. In Spain's presence he had been silent or sullenly brief in his speech. Now he had to brag.

'Why ain't you sayin' something?' he demanded. 'You act like you don't believe me.'

'I don't.'

She regretted the words immediately,

knowing she had said the worst possible thing. His face was flushed, holding an irrational anger that could hardly have been caused by her simple remark.

He reached down to seize her arm. She ducked to one side and ran downhill into the heavy brush and timber, her skirts nearly tripping her. She grabbed them in both hands and lifted them above her knees. Two hundred yards from the cabin there was a sheer drop-off into a brush-choked ravine. She heard Vedder's pounding feet behind her. She glanced back, then looked at the drop-off, twenty feet straight down.

Vedder was crazy. He had forgotten Spain's threat. He was gripped by the same frenzy that had taken hold of him the night he had beaten Frank Bowie to death with his gun. Shirley hesitated that one brief moment, then jumped. Better to be killed by a fall than to be torn to pieces by Dude Vedder.

She fell into yielding, clawing brush. Her dress ripped. Brush slashed at her face, her arms, her legs. She landed on her side, the fall driving breath from her. Gasping, she lay still and looked up at Vedder's furious face. He'd be here in a minute. He wouldn't jump. He'd find a safe way down. She had no idea how long he would have to hunt. Two minutes. Three minutes. That much time to get away if she were lucky.

She waited until Vedder's face disappeared.

Then she got up and working free of the brush, ran downhill into a maze of scrub oak and serviceberry. She struggled through the interwoven branches, slowed up until she felt as though she were making no progress. Her face and hands were scratched and bleeding. She didn't stop until she was exhausted, then she collapsed in the middle of a heavy clump of scrub oak.

She heard him coming as he threshed through the brush. She put a hand over her mouth to silence the ragged sound of her breathing. And waited.

CHAPTER SIXTEEN

Brady camped in a little draw. Most of Colorado's western slope lay ahead of him. Just a short time ago it had been the Ute reservation. Today, except in the San Juan mining area, there were few settlers this side of the mountains, few towns. As far as Brady knew, there was only one railroad and that was far to the south in the San Juan. The only telegraph line was the one that followed the railroad right of way.

A big country. A country in which three people could conceal themselves and survive on game for months. How, then, was he to find them? And how was he to do it quickly before

Spain or Vedder injured or killed Shirley?

He ate what food he had. Tomorrow he'd shoot a deer. He finished his meal and rolled a cigarette, and suddenly his face brightened. It was possible for Spain and Vedder and Shirley to live on game, but it wasn't likely they would. Not Spain anyway. He was used to making big money and living well. By this time Spain probably felt reasonably safe, having put a good many miles between himself and the Colorado line, and being lucky with a rain washing out his trail. So, before tackling the long trip across the wild land that lay ahead, he would likely hit the nearest settlement for food and whisky, and maybe an evening of poker.

Brady studied his reasoning carefully, aware that it might be faulty. Spain, like a coyote, was capable of doing the unexpected. Brady considered his possibilities. Spain could hole up somewhere, hoping that the pursuit would go on past. If he did that, he and Vedder would be at each other's throats within a matter of hours.

Spain would probably kill the younger man, use Shirley and discard her, perhaps kill her if he felt he was in the clear. The other alternative would be to go on without supplies, hoping he could so outdistance his pursuer that he could lose himself in the San Juan mining camps or cross into New Mexico. This alternative promised no better result for Shirley than the other. Spain could not afford to be held back by a woman if he planned to make a run for it. Again he would discard her, probably kill her.

The course of action Spain chose would depend upon how worried he was, Brady guessed. And knowing Spain, Brady couldn't picture him doing very much worrying. In any event, Brady couldn't comb a quarter of a million square miles of rugged country, so he went back to his original theory that Spain would hit the nearest settlement. Perhaps he wouldn't stay there, but with few travelers or strangers of any kind, Brady could certainly find out if he had been there, and probably the direction he had taken.

Brady racked his brain for all he had heard about this country in the last few years since the war with the White River Utes. He recalled hearing that a settlement had sprung up several miles up-river from the agency where Nathan Meeker had been murdered. The town, he remembered, had been named Meeker, after the agent.

Beyond the fact that the settlement was on White River, Brady knew nothing about it— neither its size nor its location. He thought of two possible ways of finding it: he could swing west until he hit the road leading to it from Rawlins, or he could continue straight ahead until he reached White River, which would also lead him to it.

He elected to continue south. He could ride

safely tonight whereas if he traveled west, it was conceivable that he would cross the road in the darkness without realizing it and waste hours of valuable time floundering around in the arid country between here and the Utah line.

He killed his fire and changed his saddle from the horse he had been riding all day to the spare which he had led. He mounted and rode south, picking his way along in the darkness, relying on the horse to find a way through the rugged terrain.

The night hours passed slowly. Brady tried to keep his thoughts away from Shirley, but in spite of all he could do they kept returning to her. Even if she was alive and well, she would be very near exhaustion. She wasn't used to riding, and it was improbable that Spain had stopped to let her sleep after the affair at the roadhouse. He thought then of some good times he had had with her, the last dance they'd gone to and a picnic they'd had, but invariably his mind returned to Spain, then Vedder, and the cycle was repeated.

In the early morning he struck White River, or a stream which he judged must be White River, and turned west. Traveling was faster now that he was on a road of sorts which followed the north bank of the stream. The sky turned gray in the east and the sun came up, but in spite of the greater speed he was making, the miles dropped behind with maddening slowness.

In mid-morning he saw the town ahead. Not much of a settlement, he discovered, but there were a couple of saloons, a general store, a blacksmith shop, and a collection of log houses.

He rode in, studying the street warily, and reined up in front of the store, a false-fronted log building with benches on both sides of the door. A couple of old men idled on the benches. They looked at him curiously, returning his greeting with monosyllabic grunts.

The storekeeper started violently when Brady stepped inside. His face turned pale, he licked his lips, and refused to meet Brady's eyes. He turned toward the back, stopping only when Brady asked, 'What's biting you, mister?'

'Nothing. What'll you have?'

Brady gave him a list of supplies, then watched the storekeeper as he began putting up the order. He moved to the opposite side of the long room to the section devoted to saddles and picked out a used packsaddle, a couple of panniers, a horsehair pad and fifty feet of lashing rope.

He carried them outside and put the packsaddle on his spare horse. He threw the rope on the ground and took the panniers back inside. One of the old men was gone. The other was studiously packing a pipe.

Brady felt the warning touch of uneasiness.

150

The old men had looked at him in a peculiar manner. So had the storekeeper. He brushed the thought aside, decided he was getting jumpy. Lee Spain would certainly have no friends here.

He packed the items he had ordered into the panniers so the weight would be equally distributed. He carried them outside, hung them on the packsaddle and lashed them down. The storekeeper came to the door to watch.

'Yours the only store in town?' Brady asked.

The man nodded.

Brady described Spain, then said, 'Have you seen him yesterday? Or today?'

The man shook his head vigorously, too vigorously. 'Haven't seen no strangers for a week or more.'

Brady was sure the fellow was lying. But why?

'Any law in this burg?' Brady asked.

'Town marshal. Here he comes.'

Brady glanced around. A stocky, bow-legged man was striding along the side of the street. Brady turned back to adjust the lashings on the packsaddle. He still couldn't understand the storekeeper's lying unless Spain had paid him to keep his mouth shut.

He heard the marshal's step behind him, then the hard muzzle of a gun jabbed him savagely in the back. The marshal's voice was soft, 'Don't move, mister. Don't even move or

151

I'll blow your guts out.'

Brady froze. He felt his gun being lifted out of his holster. He said, 'What is this, anyhow?'

'That deputy from Wyoming was in this morning 'bout eight o'clock after supplies. The one that's chasin' you. Come along now. He'll be back. Our jail ain't much, but it'll hold the likes of you. I'm warnin' you. Don't try nothin', or I'll blow you apart.'

So that was it. Spain had guessed Brady might come into town. He'd simply covered all bets. Brady hadn't given him credit for thinking that far ahead.

'You're mixed up, Marshal,' Brady said. 'I'm the deputy. My badge is in my top vest pocket. Take it out and look at it.'

'Won't work, mister. The deputy told me how you got ahold of that.'

'How did I work it?'

'Ambushed him, that's how. Killed his horse and took the badge off him while he was out cold from the fall.'

Brady's muscles tensed. He couldn't let the marshal jail him. By the time the marshal sent someone north to Bear Dance and verified Brady's identity, Spain would be hundreds of miles away. Shirley would be dead, and the trail would be too cold to follow. But the marshal was stubborn and maybe not overbright. Brady couldn't see any chance of convincing him that he was who he said he was.

'Hey,' the storekeeper whined, 'don't I get paid for them supplies?'

Brady made a slow turn so that he faced the storekeeper. The marshal had backed up two steps, his gun still covering Brady.

'I was going to have you charge them to Bear County,' Brady said, 'but as long as you dispute who I am, I guess I'll have to pay you.'

Brady reached for his pocket, but the marshal said quickly, 'I'll do it.'

Brady shrugged. 'Go ahead.'

The marshal reached into Brady's pocket and took out a buckskin bag of gold. The storekeeper said, 'Thirty-seven dollars and forty-two cents.'

Brady glanced at him wryly. 'Price went up when the marshal stuck his gun in my back, didn't it?'

'Take it or leave it.'

'Maybe I'll just leave it,' Brady said. 'Guess I won't have much use for it in jail, anyhow.'

The marshal glanced from one to the other impatiently, his gun in one hand, the gold in the other. 'Make up your minds.'

'Mebbe I am a mite high,' the storekeeper said, suddenly worried that he would lose a sale. 'Make it an even thirty.'

'Pay him,' Brady said.

The marshal stepped back warily and holstered his gun. He poured the gold out of the sack into his right hand and began to count it out. Brady dived at him. The marshal dropped the gold and grabbed for his gun.

Brady hit him low, just above the knees. The marshal went back, scrambling as he tried to keep his balance. His right hand that had grabbed for his gun went out in an automatic reflex to break his fall.

Brady grabbed his wrist and twisted. With his other hand he jerked his own gun out of the marshal's belt, rammed the muzzle into the marshal's side, then eased the marshal's revolver out of the holster and threw it across the street.

Getting up, Brady looked around. He immediately missed the storekeeper. He lunged toward the door, saw the man coming with a shotgun, and threw a shot into the floor at his feet. The shotgun clattered to the floor, and the storekeeper's hands went high above his head.

'Get out here,' Brady said angrily. 'And keep your hands in the air.'

The marshal got up, red-faced and furious. Brady said to him, 'You fell for one of the oldest tricks in the book. I followed Lee Spain all the way down from Bear Dance and you let him ride out of here just because he claimed he was a lawman.'

The marshal's voice was awed. 'So that's who you are.'

'Hell, no. I'm Brady Royal. Lee Spain was the one who showed up this morning.' He saw it wasn't any use and shrugged wearily. 'Have it your own way. Get over there against the wall. Put your hands on the backs of your necks. Move!'

The marshal and storekeeper obeyed. Brady picked up his sack of gold and shoved it into his pocket, then holstered his gun. He untied his packhorse and, holding the reins, swung to the saddle of the other one. Sinking his spurs, he galloped out of town.

A shot banged at him from the front of the store as he swung around a bend in the road, but the bullet didn't come near him. Damn it, now he'd have that marshal on his tail. The man wasn't smart and maybe he couldn't get up much of a posse in a town as small as Meeker, but even so, he'd complicate Brady's job.

The marshal could push him now, and that was the worst thing that could happen. He couldn't afford to be pushed. He had to have time to pick up Spain's trail.

He left the road and climbed out of White River valley, heading back north. For the first half hour he gave his attention to hiding his trail, then turned west, his eyes intently on the ground. He'd circle the whole damned town if he had to. He'd chance the posse, or anything else they could throw at him. At least he finally had something to go on. Spain had made a trail riding in this morning and another riding out. Brady was going to find it.

CHAPTER SEVENTEEN

Brady was fully aware of the chance he was taking, making this slow, painstaking circle of the town. He might miss Spain's trail altogether—if Spain had hidden it. He might mistake the trail of another traveler for Spain's and lose valuable time following it. He might not pick up the trail soon enough; he might be caught by the posse.

A town marshal had no authority outside of his town, but Brady knew that in practice the rule didn't mean anything. The marshal was the only law for miles around, and this was one apparently who took his job seriously and would try to enforce the law, not only in his town but in the surrounding countryside as well. He'd no doubt get a posse together and start after him.

Now Brady heard the faint tolling of a bell and guessed it was calling the townsmen together. In another twenty minutes they'd be hot on his trail. Suspecting he was a wanted killer and dangerous, they wouldn't be too anxious to take him alive.

He reined up and, dismounting, tied his packhorse to a tree. He hated to leave the animal and all his supplies, but he had no choice. If the posse jumped him, the pack animal would only slow him down.

Here the land was more sparsely timbered than it was to the south. Sage brush, nearly as high as his horse, slowed him down. Clumps of scrub oak, the branches so entwined as to be almost impassable, dotted the way ahead.

Urgency prodded him, but he deliberately forced himself to take his time. Finding a trail would be fairly easy if time wasn't so short; finding it under this kind of pressure was another matter.

The odds against him were growing. Not only must he find and take Spain and Vedder, but he had to do it in spite of the posse. In spite of Courtney and Lund too, who were very likely somewhere in the country.

From the rocky top of a high ridge he looked back down at the town in the valley below him. The marshal was riding out at the head of a posse, five of them altogether. The marshal took the road up-country, his eyes on the ground. He spotted the place where Brady had left the road and turned off, following Brady's trail.

Brady moved off the ridge and continued his search. He crossed many trails—those of deer and elk, of cattle, and occasionally the trail of a ridden horse. Each time he stopped and studied the ground carefully. The posse was drawing steadily closer. Now and then when the wind was right he heard the marshal's voice as he shouted orders to one of his men.

157

Brady refused to hurry, although the pressure to do so was growing within him. Painstakingly and carefully he continued his search. The posse was less than half a mile away when Brady found a trail which he thought might be Spain's.

He swung off his horse and knelt beside the tracks. He judged they were several hours old, probably having been made not long after dawn. The rider had been on his way to town. The time and direction were right. It seemed logical to gamble, so he mounted and began to backtrack along the faintly defined trail.

Spain might decide not to return to Shirley and Vedder. He had his supplies now and he could eat well, so it was possible, even probable, that he would abandon them and head south. But if this was the right trail, it would lead Brady to where he had left Shirley and Vedder.

Damn the man. He had added another error to those he must answer for. He'd had no business leaving Shirley with Vedder. He knew what Vedder was. He'd known before he left the jail in Bear Dance.

Brady lifted his horse to a trot and sometimes to a lope. The posse stopped closing the distance and even began to fall behind. Brady tried to stay hidden by brush and the contours of the land, and at times he succeeded, but more often than not he failed because he had to follow trail, risk being seen, risk the posse being able to abandon his own trail and follow him by sight.

Climbing out of a wide ravine, he heard a shout behind him. Looking back, he saw the posse spurring horses down the opposite slope. Now they could follow by sight at a steady lope while he must stay at a trot or lose the trail.

He decided at once he couldn't go on this way or he'd be finished within the next mile or two. Dismounting, he concealed his horse behind a tumbled pile of boulders. He left the animal and found a clump of brush that was thick enough to give him adequate covering. He levered a cartridge into the chamber of his rifle, knowing he had to slow them down.

They climbed the slope recklessly, riding hard, as if they sensed they were closing in on their quarry and felt secure because of their numbers. Brady waited until the range was just under two hundred yards, then he lined his sights carefully on the chest of the horse the marshal was riding. He led the animal a full two feet and squeezed the trigger.

The bullet struck with an audible sound. The horse went to his knees and catapulted the marshal over his head.

Instantly the posse reined to a halt, the men diving for cover. Brady grinned, crawled back out of sight and mounted his horse. The marshal and his men would lie doggo for fifteen or twenty minutes, trying to decide whether he was gone or not. By that time

159

they'd be far enough behind so that they'd have to start following trail again.

He rode out, as fast as he could without losing the tracks he was following. The trail seemed to curl back and forth in a disorganized way as though Spain had not been sure of his destination. He didn't know the country, either, Brady thought, so he'd started out looking for a settlement where he could buy supplies.

With maddening slowness the miles dropped behind. Once he was able to definitely establish the direction the trail was taking, Brady made a little better time. On two occasions he lost the trail, but by casting back and forth, he picked it up again.

The sun rose higher. Morning turned to early afternoon. He had not seen or heard the posse since his ambush, but he was sure they were still behind him. The marshal, if Brady had estimated him correctly, was a stubborn sort of man, not likely to turn back.

Brady was also sure that somewhere in this empty land Courtney and Lund were searching for tracks. They were primarily interested in Spain and Vedder, in seeing that neither of the outlaws came to trial. On the other hand, if they didn't find Spain and Vedder but did run into Brady, they'd kill him, knowing that would fulfill their mission almost as well as killing Spain and Vedder would. And Brady was very much aware that Courtney had no love for him.

By the middle of the afternoon Brady was again hearing an occasional shout from one member or another of the posse. Once more they were gaining. By this time the marshal must have discovered that the trail led consistently northeast, so he had abandoned following the actual trail in favor of an occasional guess, thereby gaining speed so he could narrow the distance between them.

Suddenly, dropping over a ridge, Brady saw Courtney and Lund three hundred yards down-slope from him.

They were traveling slowly up the brushy slope, their eyes fixed on the ground. A deer, spooking away in front of Brady, bounded down-slope toward Courtney, who was ahead of Lund, and both men raised their eyes.

Their guns came up and their shots roared out. Lund was a little faster than Courtney, but still their shots were so close together that one sounded like an echo of the first. A bullet ricocheted off a rock behind Brady. Another cut wickedly through a stand of brush less than a yard from his head, slicing off a leaf from a limb. It drifted to the ground as Brady wheeled and dug spurs into his horse's sides.

The animal lunged into the clawing brush. Brady bent low against his horse's neck, ducking and dodging as limbs slashed his face. He cursed angrily, knowing that Courtney's and Lund's gunfire would bring the posse

161

galloping in his direction.

The brush here was so thick and tall that a man couldn't see to shoot if he got off his horse. Courtney and Lund weren't likely to get down. If they stayed in their saddles, Brady knew from experience. they couldn't shoot accurately from the back of a horse. Even the slight movement of the horse's breathing was enough to throw a man's aim off unless it was point-blank range.

Brady thundered through the brush. Within minutes his face was scratched and bleeding; his pants were torn in a dozen places. But there was nothing else for him to do. He rode this way for what he judged was a quarter of a mile, then reined over sharply and headed straight downhill.

He crossed a small clearing and again the rifles boomed. His horse squatted suddenly and began to buck. A bullet had stung his hindquarters. Brady glanced back and down and saw the long, bleeding furrow the bullet had plowed.

Close, Brady thought. Too damned close. Courtney and Lund were old hands at this game. Or else they were lucky.

Brady controlled his bucking horse and yanked his rifle from the boot. He levered a shell into the chamber and threw a shot at the pair, two hundred yards on his left. They were quartering downhill fast, trying to cut him off.

The posse came into view back on the crest

of the ridge, riding hard. The marshal and his men, along with Courtney and Lund, had the advantage now. They were shooting down from a higher elevation. But if Brady could gain the top of the opposite slope, the situation would be reversed.

He spurred ahead. His horse sailed over a washout at the bottom of the ravine, missed his footing and clawed precariously. Brady clung to his back, giving the horse all the advantage of balance he could.

The horse recovered and went on, his breathing like the sigh of a gigantic bellows. Gunfire broke out behind Brady again. Bullets kicked up puffs of dust from the ground near the horse's hoofs. They'd get lucky again, Brady thought, if he didn't put a stop to it.

Swinging around in his saddle, he fired three quick shots at Courtney and Lund. They reined aside, splitting, but Brady realized at once that he hadn't slowed them down. He also realized that while the posse might be content to capture him, Courtney and Lund would certainly kill him.

He put the reins in his teeth and fumbled for fresh cartridges. He pushed them into the loading gate and levered one into the chamber. Swinging farther to the left, he picked up Courtney's and Lund's trail, overlaying that of Spain's. He turned into it, riding more recklessly than he'd ever done before. The horse plunged up the steep hillside in long, awkward bounds.

Fury at the helpless position in which he found himself kept growing in Brady. It was bad enough to go after a pair of killers like Spain and Vedder. It was worse to have the situation complicated by a misguided marshal and posse. But to add Courtney's and Lund's open effort to kill him on top of the rest of his troubles was suddenly more than he could take.

Furiously he yanked his horse to a halt in a small clearing and swung down. Spraddle-legged, he drew a bead with his rifle on Courtney's horse just then sailing across the washout at the bottom of the ravine.

He pulled the trigger. The animal floundered and went down, pinning Courtney under him. Brady didn't wait. That should hold them for a while; Lund wouldn't come on alone. Brady caught his horse, swung to the lathered animal's back and rode away without glancing behind.

He topped the ridge and dropped from sight just as rifles opened up again in the bottom of the ravine. Were they shooting at him? Or had they tied into the marshal's posse?

Brady didn't know. All he hoped was that he had gained a few precious minutes in which to try to get a lead. The place where Spain had left Vedder and Shirley could not be far ahead.

CHAPTER EIGHTEEN

Spain felt proud of himself as he rode out of Meeker. He had his supplies and he had lost only a few hours. He grinned, thinking of the surprise that was waiting for Brady Royal if he happened to ride into town while he was trying to pick up the trail. The marshal would throw him into the jug and keep him there for a week while he got in touch with someone in Bear Dance. By that time Lee Spain would be a long way from here.

Then he thought of Vedder and the grin left his face. He had to get rid of him. Vedder gave him the creeps. The man was a coward, Spain was sure, but he was cowardly only when he was not aroused. Once aroused, all conscious direction stopped in Vedder's brain. If he ever got started beating on someone, nothing could stop him.

Spain rode hard, the two gunny sacks of supplies he had tied together and slung across the saddle bumping heavily against both sides of his horse.

A peculiar feeling of uneasiness began to trouble Spain. Thinking about it, he realized that he should have pulled out of Bear Dance the day he rode in. And he would have if the pay Porter had offered hadn't been so good. He hadn't liked the set-up from the first, probably because he hadn't liked Porter—a pompous old windbag with no guts for his own dirty work.

He'd worked before for men he hadn't liked. That hadn't been enough to make him ride out, but he'd had a hunch about the deal and he should have obeyed it. Everything had gone wrong, beginning when Van Schoen's wife and kid happened to witness his killing of Van Schoen. What should have been a single, simple killing had grown to three. Then, because Porter had been stupid enough to pick a twisted guy like Vedder to break Spain out of jail, Sheriff Bowie had died.

Brady Royal had reason to hate him. The first time Royal brought him in it was just a job Royal was hired to do. It was very different now. Royal's pursuit was personal. If it hadn't been, he wouldn't have crossed the state line into Colorado, where he had no authority. The reasons for it becoming personal were simple enough: Frank Bowie had been Royal's friend. Royal was in love with Shirley Ord.

What really surprised and disappointed Spain was that Royal had started after him when he knew Spain had taken Shirley as a hostage. He probably wouldn't have if Vedder hadn't been along. But after seeing Sheriff Bowie's body, he had known as anyone would what might happen to Shirley.

The uneasiness in Spain increased. He shouldn't have left Shirley with Vedder. He had warned Vedder what would happen to him if he harmed Shirley, and he'd left, hoping, that had been enough to guarantee the girl's safety. It would have been if Vedder was a normal man, but he wasn't. Most important, Spain realized he had overlooked the possibility that Shirley would defy Vedder or taunt him, and then anything could happen . . .

He was relieved when the cabin came into sight and he saw the picketed horses quietly grazing. The scene looked peaceful and normal, then he stiffened in his saddle. No smoke rose from the tin chimney. Nothing stirred.

Spain kicked his horse into a lope and hurried up to the door. He swung down and ran inside. The cabin was empty. This was exactly what he had been afraid he'd find. He stopped, breathing hard, knowing that his uneasiness had been justified.

With his nerves screaming for action, he forced himself to stand quietly in the center of the cabin and look around. No sign of a struggle. No blood. At least that was encouraging.

Spain knew at once he was deceiving himself, realized how great a mistake he had made in leaving the girl here with Vedder. He should have known better. He had overestimated his reputation and the fear he thought he had inspired in Vedder.

All Shirley had to do was to say the wrong

thing. Once aroused, Vedder's desires would not be satisfied the way an ordinary man's would be. He had to kill, then batter and wallow in the killing.

For an instant Spain was tempted to mount his horse and ride away. Usually a calm and self-contained man, Spain felt the threat of panic. He had a feeling that things had not stopped going wrong, that they would continue to go wrong until the end, until he was dead.

Scowling, he paced back and forth. He'd better cast around until he found Vedder's trail, then follow it until he found Vedder. If he killed Vedder, and if Shirley was still alive, this might turn out all right after all. He'd fix it so Royal would discover Vedder's body, then Royal might believe Spain would release her when he was safely away. Royal might believe he was endangering her more by following than by trusting in Spain's word. But with Vedder alive . . .

Abruptly Spain turned and strode outside. Examining the ground, he found marks he hadn't noticed before. They told a story he could plainly read. Shirley had run from the cabin, with Vedder close behind.

Again panic threatened him. There wasn't a chance in a hundred that Shirley was still alive. These tracks were several hours old. Their edges were blurred by the hot wind that had been blowing all morning. Spain doubted if he'd been gone more than a few minutes

168

before Vedder had made his pass at the girl.

All those hours, beginning with Shirley fleeing from Vedder, and Vedder following her like some kind of bloodthirsty animal. Spain was certain he'd find her body close to the cabin—maybe not more than a quarter of a mile away. But he had to find her—had to know. If she was dead, the only thing he could do was to hole up and wait for Royal and ambush him. If he didn't, Royal would follow Spain like a shadow, no matter where he went, no matter how long it took.

The trail led straight into the heavy brush. It faded out on the carpet of leaves and grass, and Spain was forced to follow by guess and by studying the brush for broken, bent, or disturbed branches.

He worked downhill to the drop-off where Shirley had jumped, then he saw Vedder had circled looking for an easier way down. Spain found a scrap of Shirley's dress fluttering from a broken limb at the bottom of the ravine, and presently reached the place where she had lain while Vedder searched for her.

Following trail was, to Spain, much like reading a book. Here he judged she had made a noise and Vedder had heard. From this spot on, she ran erratically, with Vedder in hot pursuit.

The afternoon grew hot. Flies droned in the air. A mile or so away vultures circled in the sky. Had she gone that far? Spain paused, debating whether he should give up his patient unraveling of their tracks and return for his horse. He could check out whatever those buzzards were circling over in less than an hour, but the way he was going now, it might be nightfall before he reached the spot.

He felt reasonably sure Shirley had not gone much farther. This was probably the quickest way to find her body. Besides he was fascinated by the trails. Here she stopped, exhausted, and collapsed to the ground. Then, drawing on some reserve of strength, on some animal cunning she had probably not even realized she had, she had gotten up and carefully doubled back, a trick Vedder would never expect of her. He had gone on, missing the spot where she had turned, then apparently he had lost himself in the brush and had not discovered his error for a long time.

For a moment Spain was relieved. Still, he had proved nothing. Vedder might still have found her and she might be hurt and broken, abused and dying. He knew he should go on until he found her, but he couldn't bring himself to do it. He didn't want to see the results of Vedder's work.

Killing had never bothered Spain. It gave him a feeling of power, a feeling of being superior to men like Judge Porter who were actually cowards and so hired their killing done. Besides it was a business that paid well. But he had never enjoyed killing the way

170

Vedder did.

Spain began to circle, hoping to pick up Vedder's trail returning after he had discovered he'd gone on past where Shirley had hidden. Then a new thought occurred to him. If Brady Royal found the girl's body, he would return it to Bear Dance. Or at least take it to Meeker for burial. That would eat up time, enough time so that Spain would be a long way to the south. The thing to do, then, was to find Shirley and leave her where Royal was bound to find her.

A noise off to his right in the brush startled him. He froze, his hand hanging over the butt of his gun. Was it Vedder, waiting to get a bead on him? He stood motionless for a long time.

He went on, then the sound was repeated. He whirled to face it. Silence. He eased slowly toward the source of the noise. He heard nothing. Tension built in him until it was intolerable. He cursed himself for what he felt was a weakness he had never before experienced. If he was smart, he'd go to the cabin and get the horse and ride as fast and as far as he could before dark. Still, he went on.

He heard something in the distance that might have been a shot. He froze to listen, then decided he had imagined it. He'd heard something that only sounded like a shot. No sense standing here, so he walked on, still studying the ground.

A rattlesnake crawled across in front of him,

coiled and buzzed dangerously at him. He circled to avoid it. Chipmunks rustled in the dry brush, making his nerves jump.

A spot between his shoulder blades began to ache. Suppose Vedder was stalking him? In this tall brush a man couldn't see more than a dozen feet in any direction. Vedder could be fifteen feet away and not be seen.

He forced himself to forget the sound that had disturbed him. He started moving in his original direction. What he had heard must have been some animal, startled by his movement through the brush.

Glancing at the sky, he saw it was well into the afternoon. He was dry and hot and dusty. He was hungry and tired. That devil Vedder was probably lying out there in the brush some place sleeping off the exhaustion of Shirley's killing.

Now Spain crossed no trail and decided to give up, decided that Vedder was nowhere close. Suddenly, in the distance, he heard a volley of gunshots. He stood motionless, straining his ears, and presently heard three or four more shots. They came from the direction of Meeker, but what the hell could they mean?

He headed for the cabin, walking fast, cursing himself for having wasted so much time trying to unravel trails. As he strode along, he tried to figure out the shots. Royal might have gone to Meeker, been taken by the marshal, and escaped. Maybe the shots had been fired at Royal by a posse.

Or Royal might have run into Courtney and Lund, if Spain's guess back there at the roadhouse on the Yampa had been correct and they were on his trail.

Well, it didn't matter. Whoever was doing the shooting would hold Royal long enough for Spain to reach the cabin, get his horse and ride away—

A thunderous crashing of brush on Spain's right made him whirl like a cat. His gun was in his hand, blasting, before he had completed his turn. Bullets sliced through the brush, others thudded unmistakably into flesh.

Still he had seen nothing. He had fired at sounds, by reflex, something he had never done before in his life. It was possible that Shirley had been hiding in the brush, had seen him and started to run, and he had killed her.

Gun still in his hand, he stalked toward the place at which he had shot. He found a yearling doe, kicking on the ground. Holstering his gun, he savagely drove a toe of his boot into her belly, then turned and continued toward the cabin.

He had seen men who were on the run lose their heads just as he had a moment before. Those men were dead but, by God, he wasn't cashing in that way. He'd get his horse and ride. The shots he'd fired had given him away to Vedder, if Vedder was still around. They might bring Brady Royal down on him, or

Courtney and Lund.

Then, unable to hold his pace to a walk, he began to run.

Suddenly, he caught a flash of movement on a slope off to his left. He stopped dead still. Was it Vedder? No, a mounted figure. Royal.

Spain debated the time, the distance, getting back to the cabin. He needed to rest, to get hold of himself. He couldn't risk missing with the first shot. Better to draw back into the brush and wait. Carefully, so as to make no sound, he backed away. Silent, his breathing growing quiet, he waited. He could follow Brady Royal by sound, and Brady would be nosing around, looking for the girl, and for him . . .

Spain grinned like a hungry wolf.

CHAPTER NINETEEN

Shirley Ord never quite understood how she managed to evade Vedder the first hour after she fled from the cabin. Time after time she heard him or saw him go past her, sometimes not more than a dozen feet away. Each time she held her breath until he was out of earshot and she could breathe again.

The brush scratched her arms and face and tore her dress, but if it had not been for the impenetrable tangle Vedder would have

174

caught her long ago.

She moved steadily deeper into the brush whenever Vedder was far enough from her so that it seemed safe to risk the noise she could not avoid making. Twice she glimpsed his face, the sight of it turning her body cold. He must have looked the same, she thought, as he brought his bloody gun barrel down again and again when he had beaten Sheriff Bowie to death. Even Spain, a professional, hardened murderer, probably did not fully realize what Dude Vedder was.

She thought of Brady Royal in the way one thinks of someone who is dead. She would never see him again. He would be far behind by now. Even Brady, as efficient as he was, could not follow a trail washed out by rain.

Now, crouched in the brush, ears straining for a sound that would indicate Vedder's return, she told herself she might just as well face the truth. Spain had abandoned her to Vedder. He would not return. She was as sure of that as she was sure Brady Royal was still trying to find her.

Spain's story about going after supplies had only been an excuse to get away. Shirley had served her purpose, so he had left her with Vedder to give himself time to escape. He could travel faster if he was alone. And if, somehow, Brady picked up the trail again, he'd be slowed down by the necessity to take Vedder and rescue her . . . or bury her.

She heard no sounds except those which were natural in a wilderness like this: stirrings of chipmunks under the scrub oak in the dry leaves that had been protected from the rain, the fluttering of small birds through the tangle of brush, the creaking and rustling of leaves and limbs as gusts of wind ran down the ravine.

Carefully she rose and looked back in the direction she had come. She saw a fragment of cloth torn from her dress. It was fluttering from a branch like a small flag, drawing attention to itself, pointing the way clearly. If Vedder came along and saw it . . .

She tried to remember some of Brady's talk—about chasing fugitives and how on occasion they eluded him. 'Double back.' She remembered that phrase; Brady had used it many times. It was a favorite trick of men who were on the dodge, he had said. Trap the pursuers into thinking you were going one way, then reverse yourself. It was dangerous to double back in the direction of the cabin, but she didn't know where Vedder was, so it might be equally dangerous to go on.

Moving with infinite care to reduce the noise, she turned at right angles to the course she had been following. She continued slowly and laboriously for what she assumed to be a quarter of a mile, then she turned again and headed straight for the cabin.

After a slow, agonizing hour of travel she

stopped, too exhausted to go on. Besides, she realized, she would expose herself by actually going up to the cabin. If Vedder saw her, she wouldn't have a chance without this blessed brush. So she rested, breathing in long, ragged gasps, her eyes closed.

She dozed finally, then woke with a start, hearing Vedder's voice somewhere in the brush. 'Hey, Shirley! I ain't fixin' to hurt you.'

From the position of the sun she knew it was afternoon, and the faintness of Vedder's voice reassured her. Vedder had failed to pick up her trail. He apparently was wandering aimlessly in search of her. If he did cross her trail, he wouldn't know whether it was fresh or one he had followed early that morning. Her chances, then, were better. Only perverse bad luck would bring him stumbling on her.

He shouted again. 'Hey, Shirley! Good God, all I wanted was a little . . . well hell, you know what I mean. But if you feel the way you do about it, we'll forget it. Come, on out and cook supper for me. I won't bother you no more.'

Shirley waited.

Presently he called again, his voice thick with anger, 'Where are you? Spain'll be back pretty soon. If you ain't around, well, you know what he'll do.'

The voice was closer now. Suddenly Shirley realized she was between Vedder and the cabin. She forced herself to move. Her whole body ached. Her face and hands and arms burned from the brush scratches that covered them.

She began to crawl, realizing how exhausted she was. Even before she had fled from Vedder, she had been ready to collapse. Terror had given her strength, but now even that was gone.

She lay on the ground in the brush, huddled, unable to move. She heard the racket Vedder made as he crashed through the scrub oak, heard his frustrated curses.

Presently the noise of his progress came closer. She could hear his breathing, his grunts of exertion. The sounds he made bulling through the brush seemed so close that she thought he must be right beside her, but she didn't move. If he had been moving more slowly and rationally, he would surely have seen her, but he must have been possessed, tired and possibly half-blinded by sweat, so he would have had to stumble on her to find her.

The sounds began to fade. He had gone past on his way to the cabin. He had missed her, this one more time. She wondered if he had remembered Spain's threats and if fear had added to his frenzy.

But Vedder would return, searching for her. And if he didn't find her before sundown, he would be back in the morning. It took all of her will power to force herself to her feet again. For a moment she wondered if Vedder's going to the cabin had been a trick. Maybe he was still around here, waiting for her to make some sound.

Eventually she discarded the idea. Vedder was only a little less exhausted than she was. From the way he had gone past her, she judged he was far less rational. He would probably go to the cabin and get something to eat. He might even fall asleep.

This was her chance to get as far as she could from him before he started searching again. She stumbled through the brush, taking advantage of an occasional small clearing, gradually leaving the cabin behind.

Ahead of her an animal slithered through the brush and disappeared. A dog? It looked like a dog, but it must have been a coyote. Or maybe a wolf. She had nothing to fear from a coyote, but a wolf . . .

Something crashed through the brush not more than fifty feet to her right. A bear, probably. She wondered if there were any grizzlies in this country. Brady had better come soon, she thought wildly, or he'd find a gibbering idiot instead of a woman. The thought struck her funny and she sat down and began to laugh.

Her laughter increased until her whole body shook with it, until tears streamed down her dusty face. Then, when the laughter subsided, she shook like an aspen leaf in the wind. After that she began to cry, and she could not stop. She also could not go on.

The buzzards began to gather from far away. Soon they'd be circling above her, telling Vedder exactly where to look.

CHAPTER TWENTY

Brady saw the cabin in late afternoon and immediately abandoned the trail he was following. he spurred toward the cabin, yanking his rifle from the boot and levering a cartridge into the chamber.

He did not miss the buzzards circling out in the brush a mile or so to the south. There were two bunches of them. Part of one bunch had alighted, but the others kept circling as though waiting for something to die.

Deer, Brady guessed, wounded by Spain or Vedder, that had crawled out there into the brush to die. The possibility that they circled over Shirley occurred to him, but he pushed the thought away. He couldn't give up hope now.

The only sign of life around the cabin was the two horses picketed fifty yards from it, and a saddle horse, grazing with dragging reins.

Brady saw that no smoke rose from the chimney of the cabin. The front door gaped open. He was reasonably sure that the place was deserted. If Shirley were there, she would have come running out before this, and if either Spain or Vedder were inside, he would have been fired on minutes ago.

Still, Brady was not one to take any more chances than he had to. The men he wanted might be inside with Shirley, so exhausted that they had fallen asleep. And they would feel safe, with the rain washing out the trail and the marshal in Meeker primed to arrest Brady if he showed up.

He rode to the rear of the cabin where there were no windows, dismounted, and strode around the cabin, the rifle ready in his hands, its hammer back to full cock. He stopped outside the door and listened, then, hearing nothing, he rushed inside.

The cabin was empty. Brady eased the hammer of the Winchester down, noting that someone had been here not long before. The pot of coffee on the stove was still lukewarm. He turned and went outside, and for a moment stood in front of the door staring at the miles of heavy brushland that lay down country from the cabin. Above it the brush thinned, giving way to frequent clearings and occasional patches of timber.

He circled the cabin, his eyes on the ground. Within a minute or two he picked up several horse trails coming in and leaving above the cabin. He decided that these had been made as the three had ridden in, when Spain had left for town, and when he returned a short time ago. Brady kept on, studying the ground with

181

infinite care, trying to stifle the anxiety he felt. This was no time to fool himself: Shirley might still be all right, and a few minutes from now she might be dead.

Between the cabin and the spring he discovered several sets of footprints, some of them plainly recognizable as Shirley's. After a brief study, he went on.

Then, directly in front of the cabin, he found a single set of Shirley's footprints leading away from the front door into the brush. They were plain and deeply indented. Brady judged she had been running.

A set of man's tracks followed Shirley's, and in places overlaid them. A second set, probably Spain's, followed the first two. He had been moving at a more leisurely pace, perhaps trailing Shirley and Vedder just as Brady was doing now. Both men, then, were somewhere out there in that tangle of brush. So was Shirley.

Forcing himself to take his time, Brady knelt and studied the prints carefully. He guessed that Shirley's and Vedder's had been made hours ago, probably early this morning. Spain's plainly were fresher, having been made this afternoon.

He straightened and started toward the brush when something struck a rock on the ground beside him, ricocheted, and whined away over the brush. The report followed the sound immediately.

182

Brady dived into the brush. Lying flat, he saw a single horse carrying two men coming down the slope toward the cabin. The one riding behind, Lund, had his rifle at his shoulder. As Brady watched, the rifle puffed smoke. A second bullet tore through the brush above him, clipping twigs as it did.

Brady hesitated, debating whether to go on or stop and return Lund's fire. He didn't want to kill Courtney or Lund, and if he didn't want to kill them, there was no point in wasting ammunition on them.

Instead, he crawled on his hands and knees until he was sure he was out of sight, then rose and plunged through the brush. If Shirley had spent most of the day in this tangle, he would gain little by following her trail. On the other hand, he was bound to waste time and Courtney and Lund would soon find him. There was also the constant danger of running into Spain or Vedder, or both.

The best thing was to head for the closest of the two bunches of buzzards. He moved through the brush as quickly as possible, always alert, and making as little sound as he could. He reached the drop-off where Shirley had leaped into the ravine. Later he found the scrap of cloth that had been torn from her dress and was fluttering from a branch.

At high points along the way, he checked his course. Rifle at ready, he moved fast, and half an hour later startled the feeding buzzards which rose into the air with a great flapping of wings.

They had been feeding on a doe and had her half consumed. Shirley was not dead. Not yet. He had to believe that.

Aware that the buzzards had given him away, he left the spot at once and headed for the other bunch that was still circling lazily in the air. They were nearly a mile away, he judged, double the distance he had already traveled.

Shirley must be nearly dead, he thought, or the buzzards wouldn't be circling above her as they were. Instead, they would have joined the others to feast on the dead doe.

Sun heat hammered into the brush jungle as he moved. No breeze stirred now. At the moment, the thought that Shirley might be near death from exhaustion, thirst, and hunger did not occur to Brady. He could think of only one thing—Vedder had caught her.

If he met Vedder now, he would kill him instantly. And Spain? Knowing the kind of man Vedder was, Spain had left Shirley alone with him since early morning. For hours she had been pursued like a rabbit through the brush. Spain had many crimes to answer for. This was one more—and to Brady's mind, the worst.

The crashing in the brush behind him warned of Courtney's and Lund's progress through it. They were coming fast. Brady

184

asked himself if they would team up with Spain and Vedder to kill him? They might, he decided. It would be the least dangerous thing for them.

He moved faster, careless now of noise, wanting only to cover all the ground he could in the least possible time. He couldn't afford to stop and fight Courtney and Lund. They might pin him down. At least they would delay him. Furthermore, their shots would bring both Spain and Vedder on the run. That would be the finish of Shirley and himself. Four to one odds were too great.

For the first time since he had left Pete Ord at the roadhouse, he wished the man was with him. Pete could have delayed Courtney and Lund while Brady went on to find Shirley.

He fought his way through the clawing tangle, detouring several oak brush clumps that appeared to be impenetrable. He realized he couldn't slow down. Courtney and Lund were plainly following him by sound. They were too close now.

He dropped into a ravine, and finding himself in a small clearing at the bottom, sprinted across it. A shot sounded ahead of him. Maybe a hundred yards away. Certainly no more than that.

He saw the bloom of smoke and felt the burn of the bullet along the flesh of his left thigh. His leg went out from under him, and he sprawled on the ground.

He didn't stop, but clawed toward the concealing brush ahead of him, moving on hands and knees. His awkward movement caused the next three bullets to miss. One slammed into the ground directly in front of his head. One dug a furrow into the ground afoot to the right of his wriggling body. A third kicked up the dirt behind him.

Then he was in the brush, panting. He lay still for a moment, then sat up and probed with his fingers at his wound through a tear in his pants. It burned like hell when he touched it. It was wet, slick with blood. Painful, but the bullet had merely sliced across the surface of his flesh.

Shots slammed at him from the opposite direction. Looking back, he saw that Courtney and Lund were firing at him. They were half concealed by oak brush, but plain enough to be shot at. Brady lifted his rifle, sighted carefully, and let go. He was rewarded by a howl of pain. Both men hit the ground instantly, disappearing from his sight.

For a moment Brady lay still, his breathing harsh and ragged, his chest aching. He had nearly exhausted himself, and he was pinned down. If he went ahead he'd run into Spain or whoever was waiting up there to kill him. If he worked parallel to the slope, he couldn't stay hidden from Courtney and Lund and they'd get him. He couldn't go back and he couldn't go on.

Spain had the advantage of being higher than he was and so was able to see better through the brush. Courtney and Lund had numbers in their favor. They might separate and get him in a squeeze. But he wasn't going to be doggo here until dark. Sooner or later one of their shots might tag him. More important, Shirley needed him. He had not given up the hope that she was still alive.

He got cautiously to his hands and knees and began a slow, soundless crawl at right angles to the course he had previously been following. A rifle boomed from across the ravine. Twigs cut by the bullet sifted down on Brady's head.

He froze, waited a moment, and then went on. Again the rifle boomed, but this time Brady was ready for it. He fired instantly at the smoke. He heard the unmistakable sound of his bullet striking solid flesh, then someone began to groan with pain.

The first wound he had inflicted on them may well have been no more serious than his own, he thought. But this one—this one had put either Courtney or Lund out of the fight for good.

He lunged to his feet and, running in a crouch, covered more than a hundred yards before the gun on the slope began to bark again. He dropped flat on his belly at once, smiling grimly. He had a chance now. The injured man had required the attention of the other one, diverting him from Brady. That was exactly what Brady had counted on, and it gave him the chance to put another hundred yards between them.

He looked up-slope, trying to penetrate the brush with his eyes. No use. But if he couldn't see Spain, maybe Spain couldn't see him if he kept low. He doubted if either Courtney or Lund, whichever hadn't been tagged, would follow him immediately. Unless the wounded man was dead, the other one would likely stay and tie up his wound.

Keeping low, Brady began to crawl. In spite of his effort to be silent, he made some noise in the brush. But he kept the sounds as soft as he could, knowing that the farther he went, the dimmer the sounds would be to Spain, and Courtney and Lund, if both were still alive.

Spain's bullets probed for him, but missed by several feet. Spain apparently was shooting by sound, and not by sight. Unless Brady had to cross a clearing, he should make it.

He traveled for about three hundred yards, slowly and laboriously, then eased up into a standing position. He saw nothing, heard no movement. The slope might have been deserted. Overhead the sun, far to the west now, still beat down with merciless July heat.

Half crouching, Brady went on quickly, climbing up the long slope. From where he was now, the crest of the ridge hid the circling buzzards. Or did it? Maybe they were on the ground. It must have been thirty minutes since he had seen them.

A rifle opened up again behind him, but by this time the range was impossibly long. Barring a lucky shot, there wasn't much danger of his being hit.

But what about Spain? He was sly and dangerous. He hadn't stayed put, that was sure. Even now he was probably angling toward Brady, and when he caught sight of him he wouldn't hesitate.

And there was Vedder, not as tough a man as Spain, but still a dangerous one, the kind who would be like a rattler lying in the trail. He would know that his only chance of staying alive was to kill Brady Royal.

CHAPTER TWENTY-ONE

Brady's breath was gone by the time he reached the crest of the first ridge. He stopped, panting hard. The buzzards were still circling, but they were lower than they had been the last time he had seen them.

As he watched, their great wings suddenly began to beat the air, and they lifted, rising higher and higher. Brady began to run, down a short slope and up a long slant that lay beyond. Someone had frightened the buzzards. It couldn't be Courtney or Lund. It couldn't be

Spain, if that had been Spain shooting at him. So, unless it was Shirley who might have started moving again, it had to be Dude Vedder.

Brady forced himself to stop some hundred yards short of his destination. Gradually his hands steadied. He moved forward like a stalking cat.

He heard a sudden threshing ahead of him, the wild, frantic sound one hears when a predator attacks his prey. And suddenly he heard a high-pitched sound that both unnerved and relieved him. It was Shirley's scream.

She was alive.

Every nerve in Brady called for action, but he couldn't allow himself to be stampeded. Too much depended on his staying alive. He moved on, being careful not to make any noise, or so little that it would be covered by the sounds of struggle ahead.

The hundred yards seemed like a hundred miles. The minute or so that it took him to cover it seemed like an hour. Then he was in a small clearing and saw them. Vedder was slapping her. As Brady leaped across the clearing, Vedder struck Shirley in the neck with his fist. She went limp, moaning.

Brady had not been able to use his gun, with the girl between him and Vedder. Now he forgot he had a gun, everything in his mind blotted out by the red haze of fury. He seized

190

Vedder and yanked him away from Shirley.

Vedder's hand streaked for his gun. His forehead streamed with sweat, saliva drooled from both corners of his mouth.

Revulsion came over Brady. His left hand batted Vedder's gun aside just as the hammer dropped. The heat from the muzzle seared his arm, but the bullet whined harmlessly away.

Brady seized Vedder's arm in both hands and brought it down across his rising knee. He heard the bone crack, and Vedder's womanish scream. Brady released him. Vedder raised a knee, aiming for Brady's groin. He missed, but the knee went deep into Brady's belly.

And then Brady recognized something that had been struggling for recognition in his consciousness. The front of Vedder's shredded shirt was spattered by tiny brown dots. Blood. Frank Bowie's blood!

Brady's fists lashed out, cutting and tearing Vedder's face, driving him slowly but inexorably back. Vedder went down and Brady fell on him, battering him with one fist and then the other.

A sound beat against his ears again and again until it seeped through the red haze that had taken possession of his mind. Shirley was screaming, 'Brady, stop it! Brady, stop it!'

He turned his head. Slowly, the harshness and bitterness faded from his face. For the first time he realized Shirley's condition, saw how close she was to complete collapse.

He got up, staggering a moment, and wiped his hands on the sides of his pants. He held his arms out to her, and she ran to him. Her dress was torn; her hair hung loose around her face, tangled and full of twigs and leaves and dirt. Her face was smudged and streaked with blood from brush scratches.

Brady heard the sound of someone forcing his way through the brush behind him. He instantly lifted Shirley and whirled, but he saw nothing, and now he couldn't hear anything. But someone was there. Courtney or Lund. Maybe Spain. He hoped it was Spain.

Carrying Shirley, he slipped back into the concealment of the brush, moving as silently as he could.

'We're not out of this yet,' he told Shirley. 'I've got to hide you. You've got to be absolutely still no matter what happens. Can you understand what I'm saying?'

Her hands clung to him with a tenacious grip, as though she were afraid to let him out of her sight. Her eyes were fixed on his face. Her lips moved but she made no sound.

'Listen,' Brady said, 'we can't get away. Courtney and Lund followed us from Bear Dance. I suppose Porter wanted to make sure neither Vedder nor Spain was brought back alive. I shot either Courtney or Lund. I'm not sure which. By now the other one's on our tail. Spain's out there, too. They won't let us get away. I've got to go out there. Now can you understand?'

She nodded. He thought she understood and would obey. He found a thicket of scrub oak and fought his way into the center of it. He laid her down carefully.

'I'll be back as soon as I can,' he said. 'Stay quiet. Try to rest.' He paused, not wanting to alarm her, but he knew there was a good chance he wouldn't come back and perhaps she should be warned. 'In case I don't come back, there's a posse from Meeker around here somewhere. Find them if I don't make it. They'll take care of you.'

Brady moved back to the edge of the clearing where he had left Vedder, moving as silently as a shadow. Vedder was still unconscious. Nothing moved. No sound disturbed the wilderness silence. High overhead, vultures glided in lazy, inexorable circles.

But Spain would come. Spain had to come.

So Brady waited while a minute passed, and another and another. Then the silence was blasted by a shot from down-slope. A second and a third. Shots from two guns. Courtney or Lund, whichever was unhurt, had tired of trailing Brady and had opened up on Spain.

Brady moved in the direction of the shots. He was in time to see Courtney rear up from his crouched position and come staggering toward him. The front of Courtney's shirt was drenched with blood, his eyes were glassy. He saw Brady and tried to say something. Failing, he fell forward. Staring down at him, the thought came to Brady that Porter had not paid Courtney enough for this.

Brady moved deeper into the brush, listening and straining his eyes as he tried to probe the tangle below him. Spain was close. He had to be to have shot Courtney dead center the way he had.

Courtney was dead. Lund was certainly hard hit and out of the fight, perhaps dead too. Vedder was unconscious, his arm broken. The Meeker posse hadn't come yet. The odds, then, were changed.

Brady glanced at the sun. It was low. Not too much time until night. Ordinarily he could outwait his enemy, but not now, not after all that had happened.

Spain must have thought he was in the clear or he wouldn't have come back to the cabin. Now he knew he wasn't, and he couldn't be entirely sure of the Meeker posse which wouldn't be far away. Even a tough, experienced killer like Spain had a breaking point. Maybe he couldn't wait either. That, Brady realized, was the one hope he had.

CHAPTER TWENTY-TWO

Brady glanced at the sun again. It hadn't moved. Strange how time stretched on and on in a moment of crisis such as this. Spain was here, close. He had to be. Any sound on Brady's part, any movement, might bring a bullet.

But he couldn't stay this way. There was a possibility Spain might circle and stumble on Shirley's hiding place. Brady searched his mind for some trick that would bring Spain into the open, or at least force him to disclose his hiding place, but he failed.

Then, because he was unable to stand this any longer, he called, 'Spain,' and moved sideways two quick steps.

Spain didn't answer, but a dead branch snapped under the man's boot. Again Brady moved to one side as a gunshot exploded and a bullet probed the brush for him.

Peering ahead, Brady saw Spain, moving fast as he ran at right angles to Brady through the brush. Brady raised his gun, thumbed back the hammer, and threw a shot that missed.

He was glad he had missed. Spain would come to him, now that the outlaw knew where he was. Brady suddenly wanted more than killing Spain. He wanted Spain to stand on the gallows with a rope around his neck and look down at the people of Bear Dance who had put him there. Vengeance at this moment would be sweet, but not nearly as sweet as the deliberate way the law would work.

Spain must stand up before the jury of his peers and be condemned and then sentenced to death by a judge. Brady would see that he did. Dying out here in the scrub oak, Spain would simply be another gunman who had died by the gun. But if he hanged, his last struggles would become a warning to others of his kind—that the old days were gone, that the people who had settled this empty land were more powerful than the predators who roamed its mountains and valleys.

These vague thoughts tumbled through his mind and were gone. He moved forward, gun in his hand, dodging from one side to another as he avoided exposed roots and tangled branches. Spain heard him, turned to face him.

Spain threw two hasty shots that were wide of the mark. Brady caught a glimpse of the outlaw's face. He wasn't the cold, callous killer who had been brought to Bear Dance by Isaac Porter. He wasn't filled with open contempt for Brady and the law he represented. Instead, his expression showed a gambler's knowledge that this was the last hand, and that this time the stakes were higher than they had ever been before.

Running, Spain tried to thumb fresh cartridges into his gun. Brady, pressing him hard from behind, saw him stumble into a mass of tangled roots and fall headlong. The gun flew out of Spain's hand. For the first time in his life he faced death without the tool of his trade.

Spain rolled like a cat, got his feet under him and came up. His eyes searched the ground for a weapon but found none. Brady charged toward him. Spain grabbed at the buckle of his cartridge-laden gun belt, and just as Brady came within range, Spain got the buckle loose.

Spain swung the belt in a wide arc, doubled so that it struck the side of Brady's head like a weighted club. Brady felt himself falling, felt the clawing brush grab at him. The belt swung again, this time striking Brady full in the face.

Then the belt wrapped itself around his right arm, numbing his hand, causing the gun to drop.

The belt came down again across his back. He brought his head up as he tried to crouch so he could drive at Spain, but once more the belt swung, slamming against his forehead. Exposed metal cartridges tore gashes across his forehead and his cheekbone. Unconsciousness was like a gray curtain lowering over his mind.

Brady forced himself up, doubled, and dived at Spain's legs. He felt his shoulder strike Spain's knees, felt the belt beat him across his back again. The belt drove breath from him, but Spain came down. Together they rolled across the ground and into a clump of serviceberry brush that yielded and enfolded them and then sprang up around them.

A branch poked Brady's eye. He closed it, shaking his head, his hand clawing against the resisting brush. Spain's knee came up and connected solidly with Brady's jaw, and again the gray curtain began to close over his mind.

Brady was only half conscious, but beaten as he was he could not accept defeat. It seemed to him in a strange, dazed way, that his movements were normally fast, but actually both men moved with a curious kind of lethargy, slowly and deliberately.

Brady clawed his way on top of Spain and together they rolled out of the brush and onto bare ground, Spain on top now. Brady, unable to swing his fist, brought an elbow around that caught Spain full in the throat. He gagged and choked, and they rolled on over, Brady striking again with his elbow.

Spain fought to get clear, to gain the precious time he must have before he could breathe again. But Brady gave him no chance. Again and again his doubled fists slammed into Spain's face and throat. Then Brady's fogged mind realized that Spain wasn't resisting. He was out cold, his battered face covered with dirt and blood and sweat.

Brady tried to stand. He got halfway up and then collapsed across Spain's body. He lay there for several minutes. The slanting rays of the sun, a red ball above the western ridges, fell on him. Then his mind drove his reluctant body away from Spain. He searched for his gun and found it, then crawled back. He placed the muzzle against Spain's temple and drew the hammer back.

Gone now was the resolution he had made a few minutes before that he would bring Spain in to hang. He could think of nothing except his hatred of this man, of all that Spain had done to his brother, to the Van Schoens, to Frank Bowie—even though Vedder had struck the blows—and then to Shirley.

Brady held the gun against Spain's head for several seconds. Slowly his mind cleared and he remembered what he must do. Brady had learned something Bowie had never taught him. Maybe it was the criticism that had been aimed at him, or perhaps it was the simple fact that he had matured beyond his years. He rose, and dropped his gun into his holster. His hate and his reasons for hating Spain must not control him. No lawman had a right to be judge and executioner. That was the thing he had learned and he would never again forget it.

He heard the sound of riders fighting their way through the brush toward him. He turned to see the Meeker posse, the marshal riding at their head.

Brady motioned to Spain. 'This is Lee Spain. I'm the deputy, Brady Royal. Take this one to the cabin. I'll show you where the others are. If you still don't believe me, there's a girl they kidnapped who will tell you you're wrong.'

The marshal looked at him, shaking his head. 'Get up behind me. If you don't, we'll have to carry you out.'

The rest was never too clear to Brady, but apparently he led them to Shirley. Then he must have taken them to Vedder, and Courtney and Lund, who were both dead. His first clear memory was of lying on the floor of the sod-roofed cabin when it was completely dark, and feeling the burn of raw whisky in his throat.

He ate and slept while the marshal and his men looked after Shirley, who slept in a pile of blankets on the floor and occasionally cried out in her sleep.

In the morning they buried Courtney and Lund in the clearing behind the cabin, then rode to Meeker. Brady sent a message to Pete Ord on the Yampa that Shirley was safe, and another to Rawlins to be relayed to Bear Dance. A week after his capture of Vedder and Spain, he rode out of Meeker, the pair tied on horses in front of him, Shirley riding beside him.

They did not speak for a long time, simply savoring the winy, clear air of the high country, savoring their presence here on the trail together, and thankful that they were alive.

Finally Brady grinned faintly. 'Shirley, I've made up my mind. I'm going to run for sheriff. I owe that much to Frank.'

She nodded. 'I understand, Brady. I didn't before, but I do now. A man should do the job he's good at, and if you weren't a good lawman, I wouldn't be alive.'

She kept her eyes steadily on him. It was a look he liked, a look that told him she loved him, and because she did, anything he decided would be all right. Then she asked, 'Brady, what about Judge Porter? You have Vedder's signed statement. Is that enough to convict him?'

He nodded. 'With what you heard from Spain. By this time he knows I'm on my way back with Spain and Vedder, and he knows Courtney and Lund are dead. He depended on them. Alone, he's a weak man. Maybe he's shot himself by this time. Or maybe he made a run for it. If he did, he'll be picked up and brought back to hang, I'd think. But let's talk of something pleasant. How many kids are we going to have?'

'Well, it depends on how many girls we have first. You see, I want a boy. Just like you, I'd think.'

'Why,' he said, 'that might go on for twenty years, and twenty girls.'

She laughed and reaching out, took his hand. 'Yes, Brady,' she said. 'It might.'

We hope you have enjoyed this Large Print book. Other Chivers Press or G.K. Hall & Co. Large Print books are available at your library or directly from the publishers.

For more information about current and forthcoming titles, please call or write, without obligation, to:

Chivers Press Limited
Windsor Bridge Road
Bath BA2 3AX
England
Tel. (01225) 335336

OR

G.K. Hall & Co.
P.O. Box 159
Thorndike, Maine 04986
USA
Tel. (800) 223-2336

All our Large Print titles are designed for easy reading, and all our books are made to last.